Colorblind

Colorblind

A NOVEL

LEAH HARPER BOWRON

Published by SparkPress, a BookSparks imprint,
A division of SparkPoint Studio, LLC
Tempe, Arizona, USA, 85281
www.gosparkpress.com

Published 2017

Printed in the United States of America

ISBN: 978-1-943006-08-3 (pbk)
ISBN: 978-1-943006-09-0 (e-bk)

Library of Congress Control Number: 2017933885

Cover design © Julie Metz, Ltd./metzdesign.com
Book design by Stacey Aaronson

To my beloved daughter, Sarah St. Clair Bowron

CONTENTS

A rumor was afloat in sixth grade, and everyone was dying to know if it was true. Mrs. Weaver started the rumor.

On the afternoon of May 31, 1968, Mrs. Lottice Weaver retired as the sixth-grade English teacher at the all-white Wyatt Elementary School in Montgomery, Alabama. At her retirement party that evening, Mrs. Weaver told Imogene Phillips, mother of rising sixth grader Roxanne, that she had heard that the sixth grade was getting a colorful teacher. Mrs. Weaver raised her light brown eyebrows and drew quotation marks in the air with her pale white fingers as she said the word "colorful."

Next week at the Piggly Wiggly grocery store, Imogene Phillips told Coach Stewart, the father of rising sixth grader Jefferson, that she had heard that the "colorful" teacher was from the "quarter." At a father-son campout the following weekend, Coach Stewart told his son Jeff that he had heard that the "colorful" teacher from the "quarter" talked funny.

At Vacation Bible School in July, rising sixth grader

Jeff Stewart told rising sixth grader Becky Owens that he had heard that the "colorful" teacher from the "quarter" who talked funny smelled bad. At her birthday party in August, rising sixth grader Becky Owens told rising sixth grader Cathy Cartwright that she had heard that the "colorful" teacher from the "quarter" who talked funny and smelled bad had kinky hair.

At a back-to-school party for the sixth grade, rising sixth grader Cathy Cartwright told rising sixth grader Lisa Parker that she had heard that the "colorful" teacher from the "quarter" who talked funny, smelled bad, and had kinky hair was lazy.

The rumor was running rampant until Lisa Parker heard it. Lisa Parker did not giggle when she heard the rumor. She did not say exclamations such as "Oh, gross!" or "You must be kidding!" She did not even smile. Instead, Lisa Parker got sick.

Lisa Parker was no ordinary rising sixth grader. She was sensitive. Very sensitive. Lisa did not know what the rumor meant. All she knew was that the rumor was saying mean things about the new teacher. And these mean things gave her a stomachache. Lisa began to develop a sick feeling in the pit of her stomach. Lisa's palms began to sweat, her heart began to race, and a wave of nausea began to swell inside her.

"Oh, no," Lisa thought, "not another nervous stomach!"

Lisa had never had a nervous stomach at a party before. She grabbed a nearby chair to steady herself and was no longer able to make eye contact with Cathy. Cathy looked at her friend with concern.

"You look like you've just seen a ghost, Lisa," said Cathy.

Images of ghostlike men in white sheets flooded Lisa's brain. A secret society of white men dressed in white sheets as members of the Ku Klux Klan to show the world that the white race was superior.

"Are you all right, Lisa?" asked Cathy.

"Just a stomachache," said Lisa.

Cathy rolled her eyes and said, "Here we go again."

Lisa and stomachaches seemed to go together. Why, Lisa typically had more absences than any other student at Wyatt Elementary due to her mysterious stomachaches. Sometimes Lisa's stomachaches happened in the morning before school began, and Lisa would miss the whole day of school. These mysterious stomachaches would go away as soon as Lisa was allowed to stay home. Other times Lisa's stomachaches happened during school, and Lisa would check out of school and miss part of the school day. These mysterious stomachaches would go away as soon as Lisa got in the car to return home. Something made Lisa scared of school.

"I'll be fine, Cath, really—I just need to get some air," Lisa said.

Lisa walked outside. Once she was alone, she took some deep breaths to keep from hyperventilating. With her breathing regulated, Lisa's nausea began to diminish. Lisa decided to rejoin the party.

Coach Stewart's den provided the perfect place for the back-to-school party. All of the furniture had been pushed against the walls, and a dance floor complete with a Rock-Ola jukebox emerged. Refreshments were served on a skirted table near the dance floor. The room was filled with students, some of whom were dancing.

Lisa looked down at her clothes and smiled—she was wearing a long-sleeved chocolate brown mini-dress with a white collar and cuffs. From the middle of her collar hung a mock necktie comprised of brown, orange, yellow, and white horizontal stripes. Accompanying the dress were white go-go boots and a fringed brown suede purse purchased from The Third World, a store for customers who wanted to dress like hippies. Lisa walked over to the refreshment table and got a Coca-Cola from Mrs. Stewart.

The jukebox was playing "People Got to Be Free" by The Rascals, and two couples were dancing. A group of girls had congregated at one edge of the dance floor. Lisa joined the girls, who were talking about everything from boys to school to music to ID bracelets. A squeal erupted when Ann Jones admitted that she was going steady with Larry Davis and was wearing his ID bracelet. Lisa had no prospects on the boy front and remained quiet.

When the conversation turned to the start of school next week, Lisa began to feel scared again. The first day of school always terrified her. Who would be in her class? Would she have to share a class with one of the mean boys? Lisa prayed each year that none of the mean boys would be in her class. But her prayers were never answered. She seemed destined to share not only a class but also a playground and a lunch table with at least one of the mean boys. Lisa began to get another stomach-ache. Luckily, it was time to go home.

Lisa walked outside with the other students. After thanking the Stewarts and Jeff for hosting the party, Lisa scanned the line of parked cars for her father's Buick Electra 225. She found the very long white car and slumped into the red front seat. Mr. Parker noticed that Lisa seemed sad.

"How was the party, Sissy?" Mr. Parker asked.

Lisa burst into tears and cried, "It was terrible, Daddy! Cathy told me the meanest things about our new teacher."

"What things?" her father asked, accustomed to Lisa's tears.

"She said that she had heard that the n-n-new teacher had colorful k-k-kinky hair, talked funny fr-fr-from the 'quarter,' smelled b-b-bad, and was lazy," Lisa said, though her voice was choked with sobs.

"Now, Sissy," Mr. Parker said tenderly, "there's no need to cry. Why, it's as plain as the nose on your face."

Lisa flinched at the mention of the word "nose" and drew her hand across her flattened left nostril and the scars underneath.

"Your new teacher is a Negro."

Lisa touched her mock necktie and winced. She had an image of her Negro teacher wearing a real necktie and hanging from a tree in the schoolyard. The back-to-school party had just become a necktie party.

"A Negro!" Lisa exclaimed. "The only Negroes at my school work in the cafeteria and on the janitor's staff."

"Not anymore," Lisa's father responded. "Your Negro teacher is just the beginning."

Lisa's father pulled his car to the curb and turned to Lisa. He and Lisa shared the same blonde hair and blue eyes. A streetlight illuminated his white face against the midnight blue night sky. A new moon beckoned from above.

"Now, Sissy," he said, "the courts have ordered that the public schools be integrated. This fancy word means that some colored students must attend white schools and some white students must attend colored schools."

"Daddy, you're wearing your lawyer hat again," Lisa said proudly. "But what does all of this have to do with a Negro teacher?"

"Good question," her father replied. "To start the ball rolling, the school districts decided to send some colored teachers to white schools and some white teachers to colored schools. Your new Negro teacher is just such an example. It's unfortunate that Mrs. Weaver decided to retire instead of teaching at a colored school."

"But why didn't Mrs. Weaver want to teach at a colored school?" Lisa asked in earnest.

"It could be that she was just plain scared, Sissy," Lisa's father replied. "Or it could be that she was prejudiced. This fancy word means that some people think that they are better than other people. If Mrs. Weaver thinks that she is better than colored people, then she might have chosen to retire instead of teaching at a colored school."

"But I don't think that I am better than Ozella, and she's colored," Lisa explained.

"Very good, Sissy," Lisa's father replied. "The fact that our maid Ozella is colored does not mean that we are better than she is."

"Then why is everyone saying such mean things about the new teacher?" Lisa asked.

"When people are prejudiced," Lisa's father explained, "they exaggerate the differences between people in an effort to feel superior. Your friends said that your new teacher had 'kinky hair' to feel better than your new teacher when your new teacher really only has hair which is different from theirs. The mean things that your friends said about the new teacher are all examples of racial stereotypes."

"Is a stereotype a kind of stereo?" asked Lisa.

"No," said Lisa's father. "A stereotype is a fancy word for a false statement about a group of people. For example, the statement that Negroes are lazy is a stereotype because it is false—many Negroes are not lazy. Some Negroes are lazy just as some whites are lazy. So it was wrong for your friends to say that because your new teacher is a Negro, she is lazy."

"I still don't understand why some people can be so mean," said Lisa while thinking of the mean boys at school.

Lisa and her new teacher were both the victims of meanness. Some boys at school said mean things about Lisa. The rumor said mean things about the new teacher. Meanness begets meanness as fear begets fear. Lisa felt the new teacher's fear before she had ever met her.

Lisa heard a cat growl as she saw a brown squirrel scamper across a telephone wire. The squirrel stopped in midair, flicked his tail several times, and made a clucking sound. A gray cat came out of the shadows, looked up at the squirrel, and stepped back into the shadows. A waiting game followed. Only time would tell.

"I know what it feels like to be teased," thought Lisa. She looked down at her brown suede purse and silently said, "I promise not to tease or to be mean to the new Negro teacher." After making this promise, Lisa opened her purse and pulled out her troll doll. She rubbed the doll's long pink-and-white hair three times for luck. "May my new teacher and I have a good school year," she silently wished. Then she kissed the doll and placed it back in her purse.

"It's getting late—we need to get home," Lisa's father said. "Why, you've got a big day tomorrow!" he exclaimed.

Lisa momentarily forgot how scared she had been and smiled. "I'm so excited," Lisa said. "Tomorrow is my birthday, and I finally get to shop at the preteen store!"

Chapter Three

The Bra

I t was Lisa's eleventh birthday, August 26, 1968, and Mrs. Penelope Parker was taking her daughter Lisa back-to-school shopping. Mrs. Parker, who modeled before she married, was fashionably attired in chartreuse silk pants and a mod-colored paisley blouse. Before getting dressed, Mrs. Parker "put on her face," a ritual in which she applied layers of makeup to her heart-shaped face. She wore bold brown eyeliner to outline her blue eyes. Today she drove her white Corvair.

Lisa was also fashionably attired because Mrs. Parker selected all of Lisa's clothing. The Parkers' destination this morning was a girls' preteen shop known as Twix n' Tweens. Although Lisa was the smallest girl in her grade, Mrs. Parker thought that Lisa was ready for the preteen store.

"Happy birthday, Sissy!" said Mrs. Parker while driving her to the preteen store. "You know, I should receive your birthday present, not you."

"I know, Mama," said Lisa while feeling sick to her stomach.

"Yes, I labored for hours with you, and what with

your birth being so hard and terrifying and everything, why, I deserve the present, not you," declared Mrs. Parker.

"You don't have to remind me, Mama," said Lisa, "I know."

Lisa was devastated. Another birthday ruined by her mother. Lisa felt that she could never truly enjoy a birthday present again.

"And, Sissy," Mrs. Parker said, "remember that your father and I are also taking you to see the Barbra Streisand movie *Funny Girl* next month as part of your birthday celebration."

"I know, Mom," said Lisa while trying to regain her composure. "I can't wait!"

After parking the car, Mrs. Parker walked toward the store with Lisa in tow. Lisa noticed that the store's large display window featured a movie marquee that proclaimed the movie *Back to School* was currently playing. Lisa's excitement over the back-to-school shopping was tempered by her anxiety over the first day of school. Lisa was also anxious because she never felt pretty like her glamorous mother.

As soon as Lisa and her mother entered the store, they spotted Cathy and her mother at the cash register. Beside Cathy were two shopping bags filled with clothes.

"Hey, Cath," said Lisa while her mother began talking to Mrs. Cartwright.

"Happy birthday, Lisa," replied Cathy. "I'll bring your present when I come over to spend the night tonight."

"I can't wait," said Lisa. "Looks like you found some clothes here."

"I did," said Cathy. "I'm sure you'll find some cute things, too."

"I hope so," said Lisa while worrying that she might be too small for these clothes.

Lisa noticed something different about Cathy, but she couldn't put her finger on it. When Cathy bent over to pick up one of the shopping bags, Lisa spotted it. Cathy was wearing a bra. A real bra—not like the trainer bra that Lisa wore. A real bra with real cups for real breasts.

"Ratfink," said Lisa to herself while glancing down at her bony chest. She opened her purse and touched her green Ratfink eraser for luck.

After saying good-bye to the Cartwrights, Lisa and her mother followed a sales attendant to the rack of fall dresses. Lisa headed for the size 2 dresses—the smallest preteen size. As Lisa rummaged through the dresses, her mother began pulling dresses off the rack and handing them to the sales attendant. The sales attendant then began hanging the dresses in the store's largest dressing room, which was lined with mirrors.

Lisa timidly entered the dressing room, closed the door, and undressed. She looked skinny in just her panties and trainer bra. Lisa tried on the first dress—a navy blue dress with a large elephant appliquéd on it.

"Great," thought Lisa, "an elephant's trunk to emphasize my nose."

Lisa's mother entered the room and helped Lisa zip the dress. Lisa noticed that the dress drooped across her flat chest.

"It's cute," said her mother, "just a bit too big in the bust. Try the green one on next."

Lisa stepped out of the navy dress and into a kelly green knit dress with fuchsia-ribbon detailing. Lisa became very self-conscious of the fact that the knit dress lay in folds atop her tiny chest.

"Again, it's too big in the bust," said her mother. "How about that paisley one—it's not so fitted."

Lisa now stepped out of the green dress and into the paisley one. The third time was definitely not the charm. Lisa saw sagging paisley fabric where her bosoms should have been.

Her mother looked at Lisa and shook her head.

"It's precious but too blousy in the bust," said her mother.

Mrs. Parker could see that Lisa was becoming discouraged. Never one to give up where clothes were concerned, Mrs. Parker summoned the sales attendant.

"I have an idea," said Lisa's mother to the sales attendant. "Bring her a bra—a padded bra—the best padded bra that you have."

"Right away, madam," said the sales attendant, who promptly returned with the requested undergarment.

"Here, Lisa," said her mother, "let me help you into this bra."

"Mother, I can do it myself," said Lisa.

Lisa grabbed the bra and closed the dressing room door. She removed her trainer bra and then tried to fasten the real bra, the padded bra, to her chest.

"Need some help?" asked her mother.

Lisa's mother slipped into the room and fastened the bra on Lisa.

"We just need to tighten these straps so that the cups will fit snugly," Lisa's mother said while tugging on the straps.

Lisa looked in the mirror. She now had two small mounds protruding from her chest. Mounds of padding. Not mounds of breasts. Lisa turned from the mirror to her mother.

"But, Mom, aren't these 'falsies'? They're not really my bosoms," said Lisa in a low voice.

"This bra is perfectly respectable," Lisa's mother replied. "It is your secret pal and will help you fit in with your friends until nature takes its course."

In a moment of quick thinking Lisa's mother provided a bit more persuasion.

"Why, the word 'bra' is short for the word 'brag'—if you want people to brag about how you look, then wear this bra," said Lisa's mother.

Lisa knew that the word "bra" had nothing to do with the word "brag." Lisa also knew that the phrase "until nature takes its course" was a polite way of saying that Lisa hadn't gotten her period yet. Why, Lisa's mother made her keep Kotex pads in her purse just in case she started her period away from home.

"Now slip the navy dress back on over your new bra," said Mrs. Parker.

Lisa put the elephant dress back on and smiled at herself in the mirrors.

"It fits now," said Mrs. Parker. "Try the other dresses back on with the new bra."

Lisa found that all of the dresses now fit in the bust. The droops, folds, and sags were gone, and in their place were two small mounds. Lisa couldn't believe her eyes! "We'll take them all," said Mrs. Parker. "And of course the bra. May she wear it out of the store?"

"Of course, madam," said the sales attendant.

"Put several more padded bras in the shopping bag and charge everything," Mrs. Parker ordered.

And so Lisa, her arms laden with shopping bags, headed for her mother's white Corvair. She had placed her old trainer bra next to the Kotex pads in her purse.

"That's funny," thought Lisa. "I'm wearing a 'padded' bra because I haven't started my period, and I have Kotex 'pads' for when I do start my period!"

Lisa's new padded bra made her feel slightly unreal. Yet she felt so grown-up at the same time.

"I've got a secret," thought Lisa. "Two new secrets, to be precise."

Chapter Four

The Secret

Lisa's two padded secrets paled in comparison to the deep, dark secret that only her parents and doctor knew for sure. Lisa had been born with a gaping hole in the center of her face. The medical words for her secret were "cleft palate" and "cleft lip." The mean word for her secret was "harelip" because a cleft lip scar can resemble a rabbit's split lip. After several operations Lisa had a slightly flattened left nostril and scars reaching from her nose to her upper lip. She also had a crooked smile because when she smiled, one side of her mouth was smaller than the other side.

The mean boys on the playground and in the lunchroom made fun of Lisa's "smushed" nose and called her names. This teasing made Lisa sad, but she was too scared of the mean boys to tell her parents or her teachers. Lisa's girlfriends were also too scared of the mean boys to help Lisa. This teasing caused Lisa to have stomachaches, and Lisa would be absent from school and away from the mean boys.

This teasing also caused Lisa to doubt herself. She began to think of ways the children might like her in spite of her face. She wore the prettiest clothes so that the children might like her. She wore her hair in ringlets so that the children might like her. She had the most toys and games so that the children might like her. She let the popular girls copy her homework and test answers so that the popular girls might like her. And most importantly, she became the best student in the class so that the children (and the teacher) might like her.

Despite all her efforts, the teasing continued, and Lisa continued to doubt herself.

Lisa's mother also caused Lisa to doubt herself. Whenever Lisa had a birthday, her mother would relive the story of Lisa's birth and what a horrible experience it was for her. Lisa's mother would say how she deserved the birthday present and Lisa did not. Lisa's mother would also say that the only way she could cope with Lisa's "birth defects" was to compare Lisa to a child in an iron lung and be thankful that Lisa's condition was not that bad. Lisa would run to her room and cry whenever her mother told her these things, and Lisa would doubt herself even more. Lisa's father had no knowledge of these "birthday wishes," and Lisa was too scared of her mother to tell him.

Lisa's secret grew exponentially from just a secret about Lisa's face to secrets about the mean boys and secrets about her mother. Lisa lived in constant fear.

Yet Lisa had allies in the house. She had a brother named Harold whom she called "Bubba," who was three years younger than she was. She had another brother named Mark who was eight years younger than she was. And she had a baby sister named Elizabeth who was not quite eleven years younger than she was. And as her mother happily reported, these three children were not born with gaping holes in the centers of their faces.

Yet because Lisa was born with a gaping hole in the center of her face, she felt that she would have to hide her secret for the rest of her life.

Chapter Five

The First Day

Lisa awoke, and anxious thoughts immediately flooded her brain. It was the first day of school at Wyatt, and Lisa felt like she was going to throw up. "Please, God," she prayed, "let there be no mean boys in my classes."

She looked over at the new paisley dress that her mother had selected for her to wear today. Lisa got out of bed and shakily began getting dressed. When she put on her new bra, she felt as if two snow cones were resting on her chest. "If they melt, I'm in trouble," thought Lisa.

She then put on the new dress and looked at herself in her full-length mirror. "Not bad," she thought as she started brushing her soft blonde hair. Two blue eyes peeked out from under her bangs.

On the other side of town, Miss Loomis, the new Negro teacher at Wyatt, awoke. Anxious thoughts immediately flooded her brain. It was the first day of school at Wyatt, and Miss Loomis felt like she was going to throw up. "Please, God," she prayed, "let there be no mean children in my classes."

She looked over at the new dress that she had selected to wear today. It was white with a tiny print of black and red flowers on it. Miss Loomis got out of bed and shakily began getting dressed. When she put on her padded bra, she felt as if two small igloos were resting on her chest. "Hope I don't melt," thought Miss Loomis. She then put on her new dress and looked at herself in her chifferobe mirror. "Not bad," she thought as she put her wiry white hair into a bun. Two brown eyes peeked out from behind her thick white glasses.

And so the first day of school at Wyatt Elementary began. Miss Loomis's preacher, Rev. Whitney Reed, would drive her back and forth to Wyatt. On this particular morning he had much advice to give Miss Loomis.

"Hold your head high and smile," said Reverend Reed. "Make eye contact with the children. And remember, you are special—God chose you to be the first black teacher at Wyatt."

"Yes, sir, Reverend Reed," said Miss Loomis shakily.

"The movement is counting on you to do your part, so don't let us down," said Reverend Reed.

"I won't let you down," said Miss Loomis.

"Dr. King is looking down on you this morning," said Reverend Reed.

"I won't disappoint him," said Miss Loomis. "Goodbye, Reverend Reed."

Miss Loomis arrived early so that she could decorate her classroom bulletin board for her fifth- and sixth-grade English students. She had chosen the theme of "Children Around the World" to coordinate with the international theme in the Weekly Readers that the children would receive. Miss Loomis was very artistic and had made cutouts of children in their native clothing holding hands. Above the cutout children on the bulletin board were the words "A Colorful Year" in bold black letters. In the upper left-hand corner of the bulletin board was the headline "Weekly Word." Underneath this headline was the word "Welcome" written in four languages.

Miss Loomis had another reason for her bulletin board. She hoped that the white students would see the children of different colors holding hands and think that if white and colored children could get along, then white students could get along with a Negro teacher.

Mrs. Parker drove Lisa and Harold to and from Wyatt each day. On this particular morning she was full of advice for Lisa.

"Don't be nice to the new Negro teacher," said Mrs. Parker. "Don't engage in idle chitchat with the new Negro teacher."

"Yes, ma'am," said Lisa shakily.

"Remember that she is not your equal—you are better than she is in every way," said Mrs. Parker.

"Yes, ma'am," said Lisa.

"Harold," said Mrs. Parker, "don't pick your nose."

"Yes, Mama," said Harold.

"And, Lisa, don't get too close to her," said Mrs. Parker. "Negroes smell bad."

"Ozella doesn't smell bad," said Lisa.

"That's because I taught her personal hygiene," said Mrs. Parker. "I can't vouch for your teacher."

"All right," said Lisa, "I will keep a proper distance from the new Negro teacher. Good-bye, Mother."

"And not a word of this to your father," said Mrs. Parker.

Mrs. Parker dropped Lisa at the school crosswalk and then parked the car so that she could take Harold to his new classroom. Harold was delighted to find that Mrs. Watson was his third-grade teacher. She had the reputation of being extra nice and reading stories to the children every day.

Lisa also arrived at school early so that she could find her homeroom and determine whether any of the mean boys were in her class. Lisa went from door to door looking for her name on the class rosters. Then she approached Mrs. Duke's room and found her name on the girls' side of the roster. She smiled when she saw Cathy's name on the list. She then looked over at the boys' side, and her heart skipped a beat. The meanest boy in the whole school was in her class—none other than Will Harris.

Lisa began to go into panic mode—the sweaty palms, racing heart, and nervous stomach. "I'll sit up front next to Cathy," thought Lisa. "Will always sits in the back."

Lisa was able to secure a seat in the front row, with Cathy behind her, for Mrs. Duke's class. Miss Loomis was able to decorate her bulletin board before starting her first class. Yet the day loomed large in front of them.

Lisa thought that Mrs. Duke looked like her brunette Barbie doll. And Mrs. Duke had a secret, too. Unlike Lisa, whose secret made her feel unattractive, Mrs.

Duke's secret made her feel extra-pretty. Mrs. Duke was born with a double row of eyelashes. Her eyelashes were so lush and full that she didn't need to wear mascara. Yet because her lashes were so thick, Mrs. Duke had developed the annoying habit of batting her eyelashes constantly, as if she were trying to signal someone in Morse code.

During homeroom Mrs. Duke passed out the class schedule. Each student in the class had the same schedule. For Lisa, this meant that Will Harris would be with her all day long. First period would be Mrs. Duke for science; second period would be Mrs. Darren for math; then there would be recess with Mrs. Duke, followed by third period with Miss Newell for social studies. Fourth period would be lunch with Mrs. Duke, fifth period would be P.E. with Mrs. Cook, and sixth period would be Miss Loomis for English.

"Miss Loomis is new," thought Lisa. "She must be the new Negro teacher everyone has been talking about."

Lisa breezed through the first two periods without any interference from Will Harris. But her luck was to change at recess. While Mrs. Duke talked to another teacher on a far-off bench, Will began taunting Lisa.

"Look, it's Miss Smushed Nose," Will yelled.

"Yeah, did a bomb hit your face?" David Sullins chimed in.

Lisa ran as far from the mean boys as she could, tears burning her eyes. She ran to her girlfriends for protection.

Will was the tallest boy in the sixth grade, and he

had a reputation for being a bully. His best friend and partner in crime was heavyset David Sullins. Most of the sixth graders were afraid of Will and David.

Will followed Lisa and would not leave her alone.

"Your nose looks like a train wreck!" Will exclaimed. "What's wrong with you—why don't you look like everyone else?"

Lisa sat down in the grass and cried and cried. She could not wait for recess to be over.

Will did not bother Lisa during third period, but as fate would have it, Lisa and Will were assigned to the same lunchroom table. Lisa sat as far from Will as she could. Will quickly became the king of the table. If Will made a negative comment about the food, no one would dare to eat it. If Will made a negative comment about Lisa, no one would dare to help her. And Mrs. Duke, who sat at the teachers' table, never had a clue about Will and his kingdom.

Lisa was unusually quiet during fifth period. She was saving her energy for sixth period with Miss Loomis.

Miss Loomis had spent the first day trying to get her students to talk. She noticed from the start that her students would not look at or talk to her. She began to get a nervous stomach. It appeared that the parents had coached their children to have no contact with the new Negro teacher. She was being given the silent treatment because of the color of her skin.

The teachers at Wyatt were also giving Miss Loomis the silent treatment. When Miss Loomis went to the teachers' lounge, no one spoke to her. When Miss

Loomis sat at the teachers' table at lunch, no one spoke to her.

But Miss Loomis would not be deterred. She would stay with her lesson plan. She would pass out readers and grammar books and give homework. She would bring her lunch to school and eat at her desk. And whenever she felt discouraged, she would look at her bulletin board and smile.

Sixth period finally arrived, and Lisa could not wait to meet Miss Loomis. Lisa walked into the classroom and smiled. There she was, Miss Loomis, sitting behind her desk; she was so tiny that her head barely peeked over the edge.

She was a very light-skinned Negro. Her wiry white hair was piled up in a bun. Her hair was thinning, and Lisa could see patches of bald skin through her hair. Her face was moon-shaped, and her cheeks protruded like a chipmunk's stuffed with acorns. She had large lips with pink lip gloss on them, and her eyes puffed out in circles underneath her thick white glasses. She had moles and freckles all over her light skin.

She was dressed quite fashionably in a floral print dress, and her petite frame rose from its seat as the class took its seats. Miss Loomis began to talk to the class. Lisa thought that Miss Loomis had a beautiful voice and that she enunciated every syllable.

"Ozella doesn't talk like that," thought Lisa. "Miss Loomis must be well-educated. Does education take the colored person out of a Negro?"

Lisa noticed that none of the other students were

making eye contact with Miss Loomis. Lisa didn't understand, but she continued to look at Miss Loomis.

Miss Loomis said that the class would be reading poems, short stories, and novels that deal with the main character's triumph over obstacles. As Miss Loomis painted sad but beautiful pictures of what the class would read, laughter erupted from the back row. Lisa looked behind her and saw none other than Will Harris and David Sullins laughing.

"Apparently the mean boys are now focusing their meanness upon Miss Loomis," thought Lisa.

Miss Loomis ignored the boys, but her hands were trembling as she passed out readers and grammar books. After giving homework assignments, Miss Loomis dismissed class.

The first day of school ended with a whimper, not a bang. Lisa slumped home, winded from the teasing of the mean boys. Miss Loomis slumped home, winded from the silence of the students and teachers and hurt by the laughter of the mean boys.

Reverend Reed drove Miss Loomis home after her first day of school. He peppered her with questions:

"Did you hold your head high and smile?" asked Reverend Reed.

"Yes, sir," answered Miss Loomis.

"Did the white children behave?" asked Reverend Reed.

"Not exactly," said Miss Loomis.

"What do you mean?" asked Reverend Reed.

"The white children refused to make eye contact with me or speak to me," said Miss Loomis. "With one exception; Lisa Parker both looked at me and spoke to me."

"The Parker girl must be Arthur Parker's daughter," said Reverend Reed. "He is in favor of our movement and represents black clients."

"Even the white teachers refused to speak to me," said Miss Loomis.

"I was afraid of this," said Reverend Reed. "It is a white conspiracy of silence to force you to quit."

"A white conspiracy is too much for me to handle," said Miss Loomis.

"Handle it you will," said Reverend Reed. "The movement is counting on you to stand your ground."

"But I'm scared," said Miss Loomis. "The two biggest boys in the class were laughing at me."

"You must stay the course and pave the way for the black children who will be bussed to Wyatt next year," said Reverend Reed. "Just ignore the two white boys—let nature take its course."

"Yes, sir," said Miss Loomis. "I will stay the course."

Mrs. Parker drove Lisa and Harold home after their first day of school. While Ozella made snacks for the children, Mrs. Parker waited for Lisa in the den. Mrs. Parker was wearing her typical luncheon fare—a short-sleeved black sheath with pearls. Her black high-heeled sling-backs had been strewn across the floor, and she was barefoot.

Mrs. Parker peppered her daughter with questions:

"Do you have a Negress teacher?"

"Yes, ma'am," Lisa answered.

"Did you understand her?"

"Yes, ma'am."

"How did she look?"

"She was tiny."

"What was she wearing?"

"A white dress with flowers on it."

"Was she light- or dark-skinned?"

"Light-skinned."

"Did she have kinky hair?"

"No, ma'am."

"Was she mean to you?"

"No, ma'am."

"Was she stupid and lazy?"

"No, ma'am."

"Did she smell bad?"

"No, ma'am."

"Did she talk like Ozella?"

"No, ma'am."

Although Lisa's father was a lawyer, Lisa's mother had many lawyerly skills. Although Lisa's father believed in the equality of coloreds and whites, Lisa's mother did not.

Throughout this interrogation Mrs. Parker fluffed her brown pixie-style hair. Then she opened a tube of lipstick and painted her lips the color of a red Aston Martin.

Throughout this interrogation Lisa answered the questions as quietly and as briefly as possible so that Ozella could not hear from her perch in the kitchen.

"Ozella," Mrs. Parker called, "the baby's crying."

Ozella smiled at Lisa as she carried a baby bottle through the den to the nursery.

"Now, Lisa," Mrs. Parker stated, "I need specifics on your teacher so that I can move you out of her class."

Lisa's heart skipped a beat. The highlight of her school day was Miss Loomis's class. How could her mother be so mean?

"No, Mama, no!" Lisa pleaded. "Please don't move me. Miss Loomis is a great teacher. We are going to read some great books. Please don't move me, Mama!"

"Well, don't fret, Sissy," said Mrs. Parker. "I was just

trying to help—I won't change you now, but if you start having problems, I will yank you out of that Negress's class in a heartbeat. And not a word of this to your father."

Lisa hated it when her mother kept secrets from her father. Usually, the secrets revolved around clothing or shoe purchases. But secrets about the new Negro teacher—that was something new. Why, Lisa's father had Negro clients, and he always taught Lisa to treat Negroes with respect. Lisa was confused.

"Oh, Sissy," Mrs. Parker added, "I know why the school board chose a light-skinned Negress. That mulatto, or 'high yellow,' teacher of yours is part white and is smarter than dark-skinned Negroes."

"Mother," Lisa smarted, "that's not true. Ozella is just as smart as Miss Loomis in her own way."

"Well, I never heard such poppycock," snorted Mrs. Parker, who took her shoes and purse and marched out of the room.

Lisa ran to the nursery to see her baby sister and Ozella. Ozella knew about the mean boys, and Ozella's lemon drop hugs comforted Lisa like no other hugs could. Lisa thought that Ozella smelled like lemon drops, Lisa's favorite candy. When Lisa would pop a lemon drop into her mouth, the sour flavor would cause her mouth to pucker. The sweet flavor that followed would soften the sourness. When Ozella hugged Lisa, Lisa grasped a perfect world where sweet and sour coexisted in harmony.

Ozella was a heavyset woman with wiry gray hair put up neatly in a bun. She had big moles sprouting from her shiny black skin. Ozella had extra-large feet, and her shoes had slits to accommodate her bunions.

Ozella never made fun of the way Lisa looked. Whenever the mean boys made fun of Lisa, Lisa would come home to her gray-haired friend's big hugs. Lisa would turn her face into Ozella's stocky, wide legs, which would protect her, and Lisa would cry, cry, cry, cry, cry.

After giving the baby a bottle, Ozella put her in her playpen. It was time for Ozella to go home on the bus, and Lisa walked her to the end of the Parkers' driveway. As she was saying good-bye to Ozella, Lisa saw her father pull into the driveway. Mr. Parker stepped from his car and into his daughter's arms.

"Hey, Daddy," Lisa said. "You're home early."

"Well, it's been a big day for you, and I want to hear all about it," Lisa's father said.

"I'm in Mrs. Duke's homeroom with Cathy. And Daddy, I met the new Negro teacher—her name is Miss Loomis. She's really nice, and we are going to read some great books!" Lisa exclaimed.

"That's wonderful, Sissy," Lisa's father said. "See, all of your worrying was for nothing."

"But, Daddy, I noticed that the other students in my class, even Cathy, wouldn't look at or talk to Miss Loomis," Lisa reported. "Why, Daddy, why?"

"I was afraid something like this would happen," Lisa's father stated. "Ignorance, pure ignorance! You see, Sissy, about a week ago the sixth-grade fathers had a meeting at Coach Stewart's house. The meeting was supposed to be about this year's field trips, but it was really about the new Negro teacher. Many of the fathers were worried about the new teacher, and a plan was devised so that the students would not make eye contact with or speak to her in hopes that she would quit. I disagreed with the plan and stormed out of the meeting."

"Well, I sure hope Miss Loomis doesn't quit," Lisa said.

"So do I, Sissy. So do I."

Keeping secrets about Negroes became a problem for Lisa at school as well as at home. The school secrets took the form of an essay the class had to write in social studies.

Miss Newell presided over the social studies class like a medium presides over a séance. Miss Newell had long blonde hair and looked like the character Carolyn Stoddard on the spooky soap opera *Dark Shadows*. And spooky Miss Newell was.

She dressed only in black. She wore black clothes and black shoes. She accented her black ensemble with pink makeup and pink accessories. She said that black was her favorite color because it offset her fair hair and very fair skin. She said that pink was her favorite accent color because it complemented her fair hair and very fair skin.

Like a medium, Miss Newell had more than one voice. When she was in a good mood, she would use her sickeningly sweet voice and say, "Sweet, sweet children," over and over again. This voice was so sweet that Lisa thought that pink cotton candy was going to come out of Miss Newell's little pink mouth.

But when Miss Newell was in a bad mood, her voice

would become scarily mean, and her pink lips no longer complemented her words. Lisa thought that Miss Newell's mean voice was like the voices of the mean boys. When Miss Newell was in a bad mood, Lisa would get a stomachache.

It was on the second day of school that Lisa became acquainted with Miss Newell's two voices. Class began with Miss Newell's sweet voice.

"Class," Miss Newell whispered, "sweet, sweet children, we are going to write essays today."

"Oh, no," moaned Will Harris.

"Don't blame me," said Miss Newell, switching to her mean voice. "The school board is making me give this assignment. I'm sure you know that Martin Luther King Jr. died this spring. Well, because of integration and all of that nonsense, the school board is making every public-school sixth grader write a one-page essay on Mr. King."

"That sounds hard," said Becky Owens.

"Well, sugar," said the sickeningly sweet Miss Newell, "I'm making this assignment really easy. All you have to do is write about how Mr. King's death was for the best."

"I don't understand," said Lisa.

"Of course you don't understand," said mean Miss Newell, "what with your father representing Negroes and all of that."

"But my father is a good lawyer," replied Lisa defensively. "And isn't it Dr. King, not Mr. King?" Lisa asked timidly.

"In my classroom, young lady," said mean Miss Newell, "it's Mr. King—the man was not a medical doctor."

Miss Newell took a deep breath, put a smile on her mean face, and continued.

"Now, class," said sweet Miss Newell, "all I mean is that Mr. King stirred up trouble in the Negro quarter while scaring the willies out of innocent white people. And that is why his death is for the best. Every cloud has a silver lining."

Lisa felt the very black pupils in her very blue eyes turn to stone.

"I hope Miss Loomis didn't hear any of this," thought Lisa.

"Now let's take out our pencils and paper and write these short essays," said the sickeningly sweet Miss Newell. "Why, I just gave you the answer," she said while laughing to herself.

"And, class, if you want to pass this class, not a word of this essay to anyone, particularly your parents," said Miss Newell in her mean voice while she glared at Lisa.

"Another secret about Negroes," thought Lisa, who had not told her father about her mother's questions about Miss Loomis.

Lisa was confused. She and her father had watched Dr. King's "I Have a Dream" speech on television. Her father had told her what a great leader Dr. King was, and how terrible his assassination was for colored and white people alike. Her father had also told her how terrible the assassination of Bobby Kennedy was for colored and white people alike.

Lisa was at a crossroads. She believed that her father was right and Miss Newell was wrong. If she wrote the essay Miss Newell's way, then she would be telling a lie. If she wrote the essay her father's way, then she might receive a failing grade. A compromise was in order.

"If I ask for Miss Newell's permission to write the essay my father's way," thought Lisa, "then I might receive a passing grade."

Lisa took a deep breath and raised her hand. Miss Newell nodded at her.

"Excuse me, ma'am," said Lisa while trembling. "May I write my essay on why killing Dr. King was for the worst?"

"Oh, my God, you are color-blind, aren't you? You are too blind to see what color separation really is," screamed the mean Miss Newell. "Why, you just love Negroes, don't you? I should send you to the principal's office!"

"Not the principal's office," thought Lisa while remembering the song the students sang about the dreaded Mr. Breen:

Over land, over sea
Over Mr. Breen's knee
Comes the paddle
Awaitin' for you!

"On second thought," mean Miss Newell said, "you may write it your way, but you will have a hard time filling up a whole page. Why, you and your father are nothing more than colored cuddlers."

"Yes, ma'am," Lisa replied.

Lisa was horrified! She wasn't sure what being "color-blind" or a "colored cuddler" was, but she was too scared to ask her father. Miss Newell's threat of not passing her class made Lisa keep the classroom essay and Miss Newell's mean words a secret.

But Miss Newell knew what these words meant. She knew that the phrases "color-blind" and "colored cuddler" were code for the racially offensive phrase "nigger lover." And she knew that the scientific phrase "color separation" was code for the dreaded word "segregation."

Lisa couldn't wait to get out of Miss Newell's class. She wrote her essay on how the killing of Dr. King was for the worst and handed it in to Miss Newell. The essays would be sent to the school board, and an award for the best essay would be given at the end of the school year.

"My father would be proud of me," thought Lisa as she beamed.

When Lisa got home from school that day, she couldn't wait to go see her friend Katie. Katie was a grown woman who just happened to be a midget. Katie ran a one-room country store that was located at the end of Lisa's street. The store carried beef jerky, pickles, cheese, and cigarettes for adults. But most importantly, the store carried rows and rows of candy for the children.

Katie stood on a wooden platform behind the counters so that she could reach to give the customers their purchases and their change. Lisa and Harold went to visit Katie as often as they could.

"Come on, Bubba," yelled Lisa. "Let's go to Katie's."

Harold slipped off the barstool in the den and grinned.

"Let me get a penny out of my piggy bank, Sissy."

"Don't bother, Bubba," said Lisa. "I've got two pennies in my coin purse."

Candy at Katie's cost a penny apiece, and the Parker children were allowed to buy one piece of candy each.

"Let's go," said Harold as the two went outside to their bikes.

Lisa had a green girl's bike with wire baskets flanking the back tire. Harold had a Schwinn Stingray boy's bicycle in lemon yellow with monkey handlebars and a yellow banana seat. The two mounted their bikes and began the slow climb up the steep hill to Katie's. Like Lisa, Harold had blonde hair and blue eyes. Unlike Lisa, Harold was not in a hurry to do anything—even to buy candy. While Lisa was hurriedly pedaling her bike to make it up the hill, Harold was taking his sweet time, looking at the neighbors' houses and fussing at the neighbors' dogs.

"Hurry up, Bubba, you'll never make it up the hill," yelled Lisa. "Stand up and pedal hard!"

"I'll get there when I get there," said Harold matter-of-factly.

"I'll wait for you at the top," said Lisa.

Harold was busy fussing with the Thompson's standard schnauzer.

"Stay, Trixie, stay," said Harold. "Bad dog, Trixie."

The very large salt-and-pepper colored dog had blocked Harold in the middle of the street. The dog had her front paws straddling Harold's handlebars. Harold began to cry, and Mrs. Thompson came into the street and fetched Trixie.

"Sorry, Harold," said Mrs. Thompson. "I'm putting Trixie inside—she won't bother you again."

"Thank you," said Harold meekly.

Harold began to climb the hill on his bike. He stood up and pedaled hard, like Lisa said. When he made it to the top, there was Lisa waiting for him.

"You did it, Bubba, you did it!" praised Lisa.

"I'm ready for my candy now, Sissy," said Harold.

"Follow me—we're almost there," said Lisa.

The two made the short journey to Katie's, parked their bikes, and went inside.

Katie's was crowded this afternoon. A man bought some beef jerky; a lady bought some cigarettes; and the Boswell twins bought two pieces of sour apple bubble gum.

Katie was holding court atop her platform. She was no more than three feet tall. Her small head was that of a young woman. Her girlish torso boasted a woman's bosom, and elfin arms sprouted a woman's hands and polished fingernails.

Lisa and Harold could not reach the top of the counter, and Katie could not reach the bottom of the counter. They transacted business somewhere in the middle.

Lisa always felt safe at Katie's. Lisa would never make fun of Katie's small size, and Katie would never make fun of Lisa's face. They understood each other very well.

"Hi, Lisa; hi, Harold," said Katie. "Did you ride all the way up the hill just to see me?"

"Yes, ma'am, we did," said Lisa.

"I almost got bit by the Thompson's dog, Trixie," announced Harold.

"Goodness gracious, Harold," said Katie. "That dog is almost as big as you!"

"I know," said Harold. "There ought to be a law or something."

Everyone in the store chuckled. Harold loved to sound like his lawyer-father.

Harold and Lisa began eyeing the candy.

"Oh, what's the use, Bubba? We always get the same thing," said Lisa.

"Banana taffy for Lisa and an Atomic FireBall for Harold," said Katie proudly.

Lisa and Harold picked out their two pieces of candy from the bins in front of them.

"That'll be two cents," said Katie.

Lisa retrieved two pennies from the coin purse around her neck and gave them to Katie.

The pennies looked large in Katie's short fingers.

"Thank you, children, and come again! And Harold, be careful out there!" said Katie.

The two children carried their prized confections outside. They unwrapped their pieces of candy and put them in their mouths. Lisa began to chew her piece of taffy while Harold began to suck his Atomic FireBall. They kicked up their kickstands and got back on their bikes for the oh-so-much easier downhill ride home. No more dragons to slay or mean dogs to tame. Just little brother and baby sister to play with at home.

Lisa's teacher troubles continued in math class with Mrs. Darren. Mrs. Darren was a tall, slender woman with red hair and green eyes. Lisa thought that Mrs. Darren looked like Wilma Flintstone. And Stone Age she might have been.

Mrs. Darren was from a small town in south Alabama. She was intimidated by the "city children" at Wyatt, and she did everything possible to make the Wyatt students like her. For example, Mrs. Darren made her classes "easy" by focusing on addition and subtraction, multiplication and division. She did not even use the sixth-grade math books in her classes.

Mrs. Darren, moreover, did not assign homework to her students. And her students liked her. Yet Mrs. Darren's "easy" class came at a price. And that price took the form of another teacher secret.

"Class," Mrs. Darren would say, "if you want a good grade, then you must not tell your parents what we study every day. And for goodness sakes, don't tell them that I don't give homework."

"Not another teacher secret," thought Lisa. "Why, I've got so many secrets to keep that I can hardly concentrate on my schoolwork."

But Lisa kept this secret just as she kept all the others. Lisa loved math, however, so she taught herself the lessons in her math textbook and did the homework as if she had a regular math teacher and not the "popular" Mrs. Darren.

Yet somewhere between addition and subtraction, Mrs. Darren lost control of her class. Will and David sat in the back row shooting spitballs at everyone, including Mrs. Darren. Becky and Cathy played tic-tac-toe. No one was paying attention to the teacher.

So Mrs. Darren thought of a plan. A humorous plan. She would tell jokes about her small-town life to make the students listen to her and laugh with her. She would regain control of her class and continue her reign as the most "popular" teacher at Wyatt. She began by telling jokes about the old men playing dominoes. But no one laughed. She then told jokes about the nursing home. But no one laughed. Then she told jokes about the funeral home. But no one laughed.

Mrs. Darren became desperate. And then she remembered Miss Henrietta Grimes. Miss Grimes was born with a cleft palate and cleft lip, and she did not speak very well. When Mrs. Darren was a child, she and the other children in the small town would mimic the way Miss Grimes talked.

"Of course," thought Mrs. Darren, "I'll mimic the old harelip Miss Grimes, and the children will love me!"

And so on the second week of school, Mrs. Darren began to mimic Miss Grimes's speech to Lisa's class.

"Attention, class," said Mrs. Darren. "I have a really funny story to tell you this morning."

The class continued to run amok.

"Class," Mrs. Darren yelled, "stop what you're doing and listen to me!"

Will hit Mrs. Darren with a spitball.

"Well, two can play this game," thought Mrs. Darren.

Mrs. Darren began to mimic Miss Grimes.

"Gunnd mawning, cwass," droned Mrs. Darren.

The class became silent.

"There was a lady in my town who talked like that— pretty funny, huh?" said Mrs. Darren.

Some of the children began to laugh.

"She would say, 'I wanna sum hunny.'"

More children began to laugh.

"Then she would say, 'Hunny buttah.'"

Everyone in the class was now laughing uproariously. That is, everyone except Lisa.

Lisa had tears in her eyes. Her hands were shaking. Her stomach was upset.

"Is everyone laughing at me?" worried Lisa. "Why would Mrs. Darren do this to me?"

Lisa began to cry. She knew why Miss Grimes talked that way. Miss Grimes had a cleft palate and cleft lip just like Lisa. But apparently, Miss Grimes didn't get speech therapy like Lisa did. Lisa didn't talk funny because her speech therapist helped her to talk normally. But Lisa's normal speech couldn't stop Lisa from being hurt by

Mrs. Darren's joke. And Mrs. Darren would continue to use this joke for the rest of the school year. Lisa was too scared of Mrs. Darren to tell her parents about the cruel joke.

Lisa would need a lemon drop hug from Ozella and a piece of banana taffy from Katie to stop her tears from falling.

I t was a Sunday in September. But this was no ordinary Sunday. This was the Sunday that Lisa was going with her parents to see the movie *Funny Girl*. The movie was playing at the palatial Paramount Theater in downtown Montgomery. Barbra Streisand was starring in the movie, and Lisa thought that she was very pretty.

Lisa was wearing a new dress for the occasion—a long-sleeved burgundy dress with antique gold buttons. Accompanying the dress were white ruffled anklet socks and black patent leather Mary Janes. Ozella was babysitting the other children, and she gave Lisa a big hug as Lisa left with her parents.

"Sissy, you look beautiful," said her father while driving the three of them in his car.

"Yes, your new dress is gorgeous," said her mother.

"Thanks, Mama and Daddy—I'm so excited!" exclaimed Lisa.

"We have some surprises for you, Sissy," said her father. "Before the movie we are taking you to Capitol Book and News and Morrison's Cafeteria."

"Oh, boy, I can't wait to pick out a new book," said Lisa.

"Yes," said her mother, "and be sure to save room for a slice of pie at Morrison's."

"Yes, ma'am," said Lisa, "I love Morrison's."

Mr. Parker drove his wife and oldest daughter to downtown Montgomery, where he parked in front of Capitol Book and News, Montgomery's oldest bookstore. Lisa jumped from the backseat onto the asphalt and from the asphalt onto the sidewalk. As she opened the door to the bookstore, a bell chimed. Once inside Lisa headed past the newspapers, biographies, and fiction to the children's section. Rows and rows of children's literature awaited her.

The bottom rows contained picture books for babies, toddlers, and young children. Then came rows and rows of chapter books for older children and young adults. Lisa was in heaven. Once a month her father let her purchase a book here.

Today Lisa found three of the chapter books that she would be reading in Miss Loomis's class—*Treasure Island*, *The Secret Garden*, and *Little Women*.

"What did you find, Sissy?" asked her father.

"I found three books we will be reading in Miss Loomis's class," replied Lisa.

"Do you already have these books?" her father asked.

"No, sir, we won't get them until later in the school year."

"I will buy them for you now so that you can begin reading them ahead of time," said her father.

"Thank you, Daddy," said Lisa.

"You are welcome, honey. Now pick out another book just for fun," said her father as he picked up the three chapter books.

Lisa knew just what book she wanted. It was her favorite library book at school. It was called *Mr. Nobody and the Umbrella Bug* by Stoo Hample. It was a picture book for older children. Lisa looked through the rows of picture books. It wasn't there. Lisa looked through the rows of chapter books. It wasn't there.

"What are you looking for, Sissy?" her father asked.

"I'm trying to find *Mr. Nobody and the Umbrella Bug*," said Lisa.

"Do you know the author?"

"Yes, sir," said Lisa. "It's Stoo Hample. But I've searched through all the children's books, and it's nowhere to be found."

"Sounds like a job for Mr. Hardy," said her father.

Mr. Robert Hardy was the bookstore's owner, and he prided himself on being able to find almost any book in print. His desk was in an elevated square-shaped space in the middle of the store.

Lisa and her father walked to Mr. Hardy's desk and looked up. Perched at his desk sat Mr. Hardy smoking a pipe.

"Hello, Bob," said Lisa's father.

"Hello, Arthur," said Mr. Hardy. "And how are you, Miss Lisa?"

"I'm fine, thank you, sir," said Lisa.

"Bob, Lisa has a book order," said Lisa's father.

"Well now, tell me all about it, Lisa," said Mr. Hardy.

"Please, sir, I would like to order *Mr. Nobody and the Umbrella Bug* by Stoo Hample," said Lisa.

"Now what kind of bug was that, Lisa?" Mr. Hardy asked while writing the order on a form.

"An umbrella bug," said Lisa.

"And how do you spell the author's last name?" asked Mr. Hardy.

"H-A-M-P-L-E," said Lisa.

"I've written it down," said Mr. Hardy. "I will call you when it arrives."

"Thank you, sir," said Lisa.

"And, Bob, we'd like to buy these three chapter books," said Lisa's father as he handed the books to Mr. Hardy.

Mr. Hardy wrote the names of the books and their prices on an invoice. He then added the prices together and calculated the tax to arrive at the grand total.

"That'll be twenty-three dollars and ninety-five cents," said Mr. Hardy.

Lisa's father reached for his wallet and pulled out some bills.

"Here's thirty dollars—apply the change to that umbrella book," said Lisa's father.

"Will do," said Mr. Hardy, chuckling to himself.

Mr. Hardy placed the three books in a paper bag together with a carbon copy of the invoice and handed the bag to Lisa's father.

"Good-bye," said Mr. Hardy.

Lisa's mother had been browsing through the

historical-novels section of the bookstore all this time. She walked up to Mr. Hardy's desk just as Lisa's father finished the book purchase.

"Time to go to Morrison's," said Lisa's mother, smiling.

"I'm getting hungry," said Lisa.

Lisa's father drove them around the corner to Morrison's Cafeteria. The Paramount was down the street, and Lisa's father parked the car midway between the restaurant and the theater. The three walked down the sidewalk to Morrison's and entered the restaurant. They each took a tray and proceeded down the cafeteria line, where they pointed to dishes that they wanted to place on their trays. Lisa got a hamburger steak, mashed potatoes, English peas, and strawberry shortcake. Negro waiters carried their trays to a table in the next room, where they placed the bowls, plates, and glasses from the trays onto the table.

Lisa walked with her parents into the dining room. Lisa's father waved at a gentleman at another table and then ushered Lisa and her mother to the gentleman's table. It was none other than Gov. George C. Wallace. He was seated with his bodyguard. He smiled at Lisa.

"Hello, Governor," said Lisa's father. "You remember Penelope and Lisa, sir."

"Hello, Arthur," said Gov. Wallace. "Of course I remember Penelope and Lisa. Come here, Lisa, and give me a hug."

Lisa walked up to the Governor, placed her arms around his neck, and hugged him. She noticed that he had thick brown eyebrows and brown hairs on his forearms.

"What brings you downtown this evening?" asked the Governor.

"Why, Governor, we have brought Lisa to see *Funny Girl* for her birthday," said Lisa's father.

"Is today your birthday, Lisa?" asked Gov. Wallace.

"No, sir, my birthday was August twenty-sixth," said Lisa.

"August twenty-sixth—why, my birthday is August twenty-fifth! We should celebrate together next year," said Gov. Wallace.

"Yes, sir, Governor," said Lisa excitedly.

"Lisa, tell the Governor about your new teacher, Miss Loomis," said Lisa's father.

"My new teacher is a Negro," said Lisa. "She is very nice."

"Well, it's a small world," said the Governor. "That's wonderful, Lisa. You children need to make her feel welcome at your school."

"Yes, sir, Governor," said Lisa.

"Governor, how goes the presidential campaign?" asked Lisa's father.

"Great," said the Governor. "We're picking up speed wherever we go!"

"That's wonderful, Governor," said Lisa's father.

Lisa noticed that Gov. Wallace was eating a hamburger steak with ketchup on it.

"He's eating the same thing I am," thought Lisa.

Lisa and her parents excused themselves from the

Governor's table and proceeded to their table, where they shared an enjoyable meal. Soon it was time to walk to the Paramount to see *Funny Girl*. Lisa liked the movie and its songs. But Lisa didn't like the title of the movie. It reminded her of the mean boys. The mean boys made fun of her funny nose. The mean boys treated her like a "funny girl" because of her nose, but she didn't feel like singing.

That night Lisa dreamed that she and Gov. Wallace were celebrating their birthdays together at the Little White House of the Confederacy in downtown Montgomery. They were seated in the formal dining room, and Miss Loomis was in the room too. Lisa noticed that Miss Loomis was wearing a servant's uniform, and she was carrying a huge birthday cake to the table. The candles on the cake were in the shape of white crosses, and they were on fire. Try as they might, Lisa and Gov. Wallace could not blow the candles out. The white candles then turned into white doves, which flew around the room trying to get out. Lisa awoke from the dream and wondered what it meant.

Chapter Eleven

The Fair

September heralded the Alabama State Fair in Montgomery. Mrs. Cartwright and Cathy had asked Lisa to be their guest at the fair this year. After obtaining permission from her parents, Lisa gladly accepted their invitation for Saturday. As the big day approached, Lisa's mother was full of warnings about the fair.

"Pay attention, Lisa, and don't get separated from the Cartwrights," Mrs. Parker warned.

"Yes, ma'am," Lisa replied.

"Don't ride any rides that are too fast or too scary," Mrs. Parker said.

"Yes, ma'am," Lisa replied.

"And watch your money at all times—those carnival operators will steal anything they can."

"Yes, ma'am," Lisa replied. "Daddy is giving me five whole dollars for the fair!"

"I know," said Mrs. Parker. "And stay away from the games—they are rigged so that you will lose."

"But I want to try to win a stuffed animal," said Lisa.

"Well, if you lose all your money, don't say I didn't warn you," said Mrs. Parker.

"I'm not going to lose all my money," said Lisa. "Besides, I want to buy gifts for Bubba, Mark, and Elizabeth."

"That's very nice of you to think of your brothers and sister, but I want you to have fun, too," said Mrs. Parker.

"I will," beamed Lisa.

The day arrived, and Mrs. Cartwright drove Lisa and Cathy to the fair. Lisa and Cathy wore bell-bottomed hip-huggers and carried suede purses.

It was a cool, crisp fall day—a perfect day for walking up and down the midway. Before reaching the midway, the threesome had to pass through the 4-H livestock section. The pungent smell of manure mixed with animal sweat greeted them.

"Phew," said Cathy while holding her nose.

"I want to see the baby pigs," said Lisa.

"But it stinks," said Cathy.

"The pigs are over there," said Mrs. Cartwright, pointing to a pen in the corner.

Lisa and Cathy saw a mother pig nursing her piglets.

"Look, he's just like Wilbur from *Charlotte's Web*. He's so cute!" Lisa exclaimed while pointing to a piglet.

Lisa had been in love with pigs since she read *Charlotte's Web* three years ago. Wilbur the pig became her imagined pet. She begged her father repeatedly for a pet pig just like Wilbur from the book. She imagined putting a baby bonnet on the pig and strolling it in the baby stroller. Yet her father always refused. He said that pigs were not allowed to live in city neighborhoods and that pigs grow up to be enormous hogs. Lisa resolved herself to a Siamese cat and a basset hound.

Lisa's favorite book was *Charlotte's Web*, and she used it for her book report two years in a row. She made a shadow box of the book complete with a plastic Wilbur. Lisa was told that she had to choose a different book for the next year. Yet Lisa never chose a different favorite pet. Why, she even had her father take a Polaroid of her and a pig at a petting zoo.

"Lisa, it's time to go—I want to ride the Tilt-a-Whirl," said Cathy while pointing to the midway.

"OK, bye-bye, little Wilbur," Lisa said dreamily.

The three left the farm animals and headed for the midway.

"Look up ahead," Cathy said. "I spy candy apples."

"Oh, boy," said Lisa, "caramel apples are my favorite!"

"Let's go for a ride first," said Cathy.

"OK," said Lisa. "I see the Tilt-a-Whirl on the left."

"Mom," said Cathy, "we want to ride the Tilt-a-Whirl, please, please, please."

"OK," said Mrs. Cartwright, "here's the money for two tickets."

"I brought my own money," said Lisa.

"I'm paying for the food and the rides—save your money for games and toys," said Mrs. Cartwright.

"Thank you so much," said Lisa.

The two girls bought their tickets and took their seats in a car. In the car behind them, two Negro children were seated.

"Don't seat my girls next to Negroes," Mrs. Cartwright yelled to the carnival attendant. "Move them now."

The carnival attendant walked to Lisa and Cathy's car.

"Get out, girls—I'm moving you to a different car," said the attendant.

"Is there something wrong with this car?" asked Lisa.

"No," said Cathy, "there's something wrong with *that* car." She pointed to the car with the Negro children inside.

"But I don't understand," said Lisa.

"My father told me that whites are not supposed to mix with coloreds," said Cathy.

Lisa hoped that the Negro children did not hear what Cathy had just said.

The attendant moved Lisa and Cathy to a seat away from the Negro children. The attendant then fastened their seat belts, and they were off on a spinning, tilting ride. Both girls were screaming but smiling too. When the ride was over, Lisa had trouble regaining her balance.

"Time for a game," said Cathy.

"Win a stuffed animal—pick a color, any color—only a quarter to win," yelled the carnival barker.

The girls eyed the game.

"It's easy," said Lisa. "You put a quarter on a color; he throws a ball into the color pit, and if the ball lands on your color, you win."

"I'm going to put a quarter on red," said Cathy.

"I choose green," said Lisa, who put her quarter on the color green.

The carnival barker threw the ball into the pit, and it landed on green.

"I won, I won!" screamed Lisa. "I want a Snoopy dog."

The stuffed animals were hanging from the ceiling. The barker took down a Snoopy dog and handed it to Lisa. Lisa noticed that the animal was stuffed with Styrofoam pellets instead of cotton batting and that the animal didn't quite look like the Peanuts character Snoopy. But she loved him just the same.

"Congratulations, Lisa," Mrs. Cartwright said. "I'll hold that for you."

"Thanks—here you go," said Lisa while handing her stuffed animal to Mrs. Cartwright.

"Let's get something to eat," said Cathy.

Mrs. Cartwright bought the girls corn dogs and drinks. After eating their food, the girls and Mrs. Cartwright walked farther down the midway.

"Look over here," said Cathy, "a freak show—I want to go inside."

Large wooden sandwich boards advertised a bearded woman, a two-headed baby, and a two-headed calf.

"Come see the freaks, the animal oddities—view the bearded lady, the two-headed baby, and the two-headed calf," said the carnival barker over the loudspeaker.

"Let's go, Lisa, let's go," said Cathy.

Lisa had an uneasy feeling. Her palms began to sweat, her heart began to race, and a wave of nausea began to swell inside her.

"Not another nervous stomach," thought Lisa.

"Are you OK, Lisa?" asked Cathy.

"I'm fine," said Lisa while pretending to be all right. "Let's go inside."

Mrs. Cartwright bought the tickets, and the three went inside.

"I want to see that two-headed baby," said Cathy.

The attraction opened with jars and jars of velvety animal oddities floating in green formaldehyde. A large jar containing a two-headed calf greeted them. The calf's two heads sat atop two necks. The calf's skin was the color of milk and looked to be the consistency of cheese. The calf's four eyes stared at the girls.

"Freaky," said Cathy.

Lisa's face was turning as green as the formaldehyde.

Around the corner from the specimen jars was the "bearded lady." The "bearded lady" was tall and slender like a woman, with a woman's black curly hair tied up in ribbons. The "bearded lady" wore a pink ball gown, earrings, makeup, and pink women's shoes. Yet the "bearded lady" had a dense, curly black beard and curly black arm hair.

"That just looks like a man wearing a pink dress," said Cathy.

"But this is a woman—she is wearing a bra," said Lisa.

"Well, I still think it's a man—besides, the bra could be padded," said Cathy.

Lisa swallowed hard. She was wearing her new padded bra.

"If only Cathy knew," thought Lisa.

Around the final corner was a very large specimen jar. Lisa took a deep breath and looked inside to see the fetus of a two-headed baby boy. One of the heads was normal. The other head looked like a monster to Lisa. Instead of a nose and upper lip, it had a gaping hole.

"Oh, my God," thought Lisa. "Is this how I looked at birth? Am I a freak, too?"

"Mom, what's wrong with this baby's face?" asked Cathy. "Is that why this baby died?"

"I'm not sure, Cathy," said Mrs. Cartwright. "Only God determines the cause of death."

"I'm not feeling well," said Lisa. "Could we leave?"

"Come outside and get some air," said Mrs. Cartwright.

Mrs. Cartwright and Cathy ushered Lisa outside.

"That's better," said Lisa, taking some deep breaths.

"There's nothing to be afraid of, Lisa," said Cathy. "That two-headed monster is dead and can't hurt you."

"That baby's not a monster," said Lisa.

"Well, it's in the freak show," said Cathy."

"Now, girls, how about some candy apples?" said Mrs. Cartwright.

"Sure," said Cathy.

"OK," said Lisa, regaining her strength.

After eating candy and caramel apples, Lisa and Cathy rode more rides, played more games, and ate more food. Lisa bought gifts for her brothers and sister—a plastic sword for Harold, a bouncy ball for Mark, and a Kewpie doll for Elizabeth.

It was getting late when they left the midway. The

neon lights made the old, dirty rides look like new. But nothing could ever make the freak show look inviting to Lisa. The freak show only showed Lisa how close she was to being a freak herself. Lisa doubted herself even more and hugged her Snoopy dog for comfort, flattened nose to puffy nose. The fair was not really "fair" to Lisa—it became a reminder of just how different from everyone else she really was.

Lisa had many confrontations with Will and David over the month of October. And many stomachaches ensued. Yet instead of checking out of school and being absent, Lisa stayed. The deciding factor was Miss Loomis. Lisa did not want to miss a minute of Miss Loomis's class. So she endured the teasing and tried to calm her nervous stomach.

Miss Loomis had many confrontations with Will and David over the month of October. And the silent treatment continued. Many stomachaches ensued. Yet instead of quitting, Miss Loomis stayed. The deciding factors were Lisa and Reverend Reed. Miss Loomis did not want to miss a minute of class with Lisa. Miss Loomis also did not want to disappoint Reverend Reed or the movement. So she endured the teasing and silent treatment and tried to calm her nervous stomach.

Yet the events surrounding the school Halloween carnival would prove to be the scariest confrontation between Will and David, on the one hand, and Lisa and Miss Loomis, on the other. And it all began with the costume contest.

Each October Wyatt hosted a Halloween carnival and

open house for the students and their families. The carnival included games (such as go fish, bingo, musical chairs, and beanbag toss) as well as a cakewalk, costume contest, and haunted house. Each teacher also hosted an open house for the students and their families.

On the evening of the carnival, Lisa dressed up as comic-book character Wendy the Good Little Witch. Her little brother Harold dressed up as Wendy's sidekick, comic-book character Casper the Friendly Ghost. Although Lisa wanted to dress up as a scary witch, Lisa's mother insisted that she and Harold have matching costumes for the costume contest. Lisa's baby brother, two-year-old Mark, dressed up as a pint-size version of Casper because he wanted to be just like his brother. Mrs. Parker bought these genuine Hasbro costumes from the variety store. The costumes and masks were identical to the comic-book images of the cartoon characters Casper and Wendy.

As the costumed children piled into Mr. Parker's car, Mrs. Parker gave instructions to Ozella.

"Take good care of baby Elizabeth," said Mrs. Parker. "We should be back before seven thirty tonight."

"Yes, ma'am, Miss Penelope," said Ozella as she closed the front door.

Mrs. Parker jumped into the front seat of her husband's car and began asking Harold questions.

"Bubba, do you have your trick-or-treat bag?" asked Mrs. Parker.

"Yes, ma'am," answered Harold, "but I'm not Bubba, I'm Casper the Friendly Ghost."

"No, I'm Cappuh," said Mark.

"All right," said Mrs. Parker, "I want both of my Caspers to hold hands at the carnival so you won't get lost."

"But I can't play the games if I'm holding Brother's hand," said Harold.

"All right," said Mrs. Parker, "but I want both of my Caspers to stay close to me at the carnival."

"But I can't use the boys' bathroom if I'm next to you," said Harold.

"Oh, you know what I mean," said an exasperated Mrs. Parker. "And little Casper, you have to tell me when you need to go to the bathroom."

"I'm big Cappuh," said Mark, "and I go to the baff-woom wif Bubba."

"All right, my Caspers," said Lisa, "this is Wendy the Good Little Witch, who says to stay close to Mama and have a great time at the carnival."

"OK, Sissy," said Harold, "you have fun, too."

"OK, Sissy," said Mark, "I stay kwose to Mama."

"Very good, boys," said Mr. Parker, "and please mind your mother."

"Yes, sir," said Harold.

"Yes, suh," said Mark.

Mr. Parker parked his car in the school parking lot and gave his family further instructions.

"It is now five o'clock. The first order of business is the costume contest in the school auditorium. Once the contest is over, you will have plenty of time to visit your teachers, play games, and see the haunted house. Harold and Mark, you will be with your mother at all times, and Lisa will be with me. We will meet back at the front entrance to the school at seven o'clock," said Mr. Parker.

"OK, dear," said Mrs. Parker. "Here are carnival tickets for you and Lisa."

"Thanks, dear," said Mr. Parker, "and remember, if anyone gets lost, go to the nearest parent or teacher and ask for help. Your mother or I will be right there to get you."

The family got out of the car and walked to the school's front doors, which were decorated with ghosts, jack-o'-lanterns, and witches. They went inside to see a witches' cauldron smoldering with dry ice and two mothers dressed up like witches. The mothers were dressed in black dresses with black boots and witches' hats. The first witch had a green face and a wart on her nose. The second witch had a purple face with a spider on her cheek. Each witch had a silver wand.

"Bubble, bubble, toil, and trouble," said the first witch.

"I think I see the Parkers' double," said the second witch.

"I see two Caspers with my eye," said the first witch.

"And Wendy too, I spy, I spy," said the second witch.

"Very clever, Imogene and Lynn," said Mr. Parker. "And a happy Halloween to both of you."

The Parker family headed straight for the auditorium and the costume contest. Mrs. Parker made it a point to enter her children in the costume contest each year. And each year they won—in large part due to Mrs. Parker.

Mrs. Parker would provide props for each child's costume. And these props would turn an ordinary costume into an extraordinary one. Lisa, for example, carried a wicker basket with a stuffed dog that looked just like Toto when Lisa was Dorothy from *The Wizard of Oz* last year, and she won best girls' costume for the fifth grade.

This year Mrs. Parker added white gloves, a black top hat, and a white stuffed dog to Harold's Casper costume and a red witch's hat, a red broom, and a white stuffed cat to Lisa's Wendy costume. Mrs. Parker felt that with these props her children were poised to win yet again.

While the prizes for this year's boys' and girls' costumes were being awarded, Mrs. Parker scoured the auditorium looking for this year's group competition. The Jones's children were dressed like Dorothy, the Scarecrow, and the Tin Man—the Cowardly Lion was missing.

"A fatal mistake," thought Mrs. Parker.

The Boswell twins were dressed as cartoon characters Underdog and his girlfriend Sweet Polly Purebred. Timmy Boswell was tugging at his Sweet Polly Purebred costume.

"They don't have props," thought Mrs. Parker.

Mrs. Parker then saw two boys dressed as ghosts enter the auditorium and sit in the back row.

"Their costumes look too homemade," thought Mrs. Parker.

The contestants for best group costume were called to the stage. Lisa and Harold as Wendy and Casper walked up the steps to the stage and stood next to the judge, who was none other than the principal, Mr. Breen. Then Margaret, Gretchen, and Danny Jones, as Dorothy, the Scarecrow, and the Tin Man, took the stage. Finally twins Bobby and Timmy Boswell, as Underdog and Sweet Polly Purebred, walked onto the stage.

Mr. Breen, who was wearing a gray flannel suit, gathered the contestants together.

"Attention, please," said Mr. Breen. "Do I have all contestants for the group contest on the stage now?"

There was no response from the audience. Mr. Breen noticed the two boys dressed as ghosts sitting together in the auditorium.

"Would the two ghosts in the last row please identify yourselves?" asked Mr. Breen.

The ghost wearing black tennis shoes said, "I am Will Harris, sir."

The ghost wearing white tennis shoes said, "I am David Sullins, sir."

"Will and David," said Mr. Breen, "do you boys want to be contestants in the group costume contest?"

"Please, God, no," prayed Lisa.

"No, sir," said Will, "we're just here to watch."

"Thank you, God," prayed Lisa, "thank you."

The mere thought that Will and David would be watching her gave Lisa a nervous stomach, and she grabbed Harold's hand to steady herself.

"All right," said Mr. Breen, "we have three groups onstage competing for the group costume prize—the Jones group, the Parker group, and the Boswell group."

With the mention of his last name, Timmy Boswell began to jump up and down. His brother Bobby looked in the audience for help.

"Contestants, are you ready to promenade?" Mr. Breen asked.

"I want to go home," yelled Timmy Boswell.

Will and David began to laugh at Timmy's costume.

"What a sissy," said Will. "I wouldn't be caught dead in a girls' costume."

"What's wrong, Timmy?" Mr. Breen asked.

"It's not fair," said Timmy. "Bobby gets to be Underdog, but I have to be Sweet Polly Purebred. I don't want to wear a dress," said Timmy while pulling at his costume.

"So, are you going to stay or leave?" asked Mr. Breen.

"Leave," said Timmy.

"Good riddance," said David.

Timmy promptly left the stage, followed by his brother. Mrs. Boswell threw up her hands in dismay.

"Would the remaining two groups promenade around the stage three times?" said Mr. Breen.

The Jones children and the Parker children walked around the stage three times. With each turn the Parker children doffed their hats and held their white cat and dog in the air. With each turn Will and David laughed at Lisa.

"Look at Lisa," said Will. "She's too scared to be a real witch."

"Yeah, she's wearing a baby costume," said David.

"At least her mask covers up her scary face," said Will.

"You said it," replied David.

"Stop, boys," said Mr. Breen. "I've had enough of your tomfoolery."

Heeding the principal's warning, Will and David got up from their seats and left the auditorium. The contestants finished their promenade, and Mr. Breen turned to Margaret Jones.

"Margaret, where is your Cowardly Lion?" Mr. Breen asked.

"Howard was supposed to be the Cowardly Lion, but he was too afraid to come," said Margaret.

"Thank you, Margaret," said Mr. Breen. "I have made my decision. I hereby award this year's group costume prize to Lisa and Harold Parker. Wendy the Good Little Witch and Casper the Friendly Ghost never looked better! Here is your blue ribbon," said Mr. Breen.

Lisa graciously took the blue ribbon and nervously escorted her brother off the stage and to their seats in the auditorium.

"Let me have that ribbon," said Mrs. Parker. "Congratulations to both of you."

"Yes, congratulations," said Mr. Parker. "Are you all right, Lisa?"

"Yes, sir," said Lisa, "I'm fine."

"Good," said Mr. Parker. "Well, Mr. Breen certainly put those boys in their place—I'm sure they won't bother you again."

"Yes, sir," said Lisa, who was too scared to tell her father the truth about Will and David.

"Children, this is where we go our separate ways,"

said Mr. Parker. "Boys, behave yourselves and have fun. Come on, Lisa."

Mrs. Parker escorted Harold and Mark to the bean-bag toss while Mr. Parker and Lisa headed the other direction.

"Daddy, this way to the cakewalk," said Lisa. "I want to try to win Miss Loomis's cake."

The cakewalk was located in the lunchroom. The tables and chairs had been pushed to one side, and two large concentric circles had been drawn on the floor with colored chalk. Between the circles, numbers were drawn with the chalk.

To play the game, a player stands on a number between the circles and then walks around the circles while the music plays. When the music stops, the player stops walking, and a piece of paper with a number on it is drawn from a bowl. The player who stands on the number that matches the number drawn wins and selects a cake as his or her prize.

Each teacher baked a cake for this carnival game. The cakes were displayed on three lunchroom tables adjacent to the chalk circles.

"May I have a ticket for the cakewalk, please," Lisa asked her father.

"Here you go," said Mr. Parker, handing his daughter a carnival ticket.

"Thanks, Daddy," said Lisa.

Mrs. Stewart was in charge of the cakewalk. Lisa gave Mrs. Stewart her ticket and proceeded to the chalk circles. She stood on number 10, her lucky number. Once the circles were filled with players, Mrs. Stewart started the music playing. The players began to walk in a clockwise direction around the circles. When Mrs. Stewart stopped the music, Lisa was standing on number 7. Mrs. Stewart drew number 5—Roxanne Phillips was the winner, and she chose Mrs. Darren's pound cake.

Lisa walked back to her father.

"May I try one more time, Daddy?" Lisa asked. "Please?"

"Of course you can," said Mr. Parker. "Here's another ticket."

"Thanks, Daddy," said Lisa as she took the ticket and handed it to Mrs. Stewart.

Lisa walked to the chalk circles and again stood on lucky number 10. Will and David walked into the lunchroom and stood in the background, watching Lisa. Lisa immediately became ill at ease. Mrs. Stewart started the music, and Lisa cautiously marched around the circles. When the music stopped, Lisa was on lucky number 10. Mrs. Stewart then drew number 10, and Lisa was the winner.

"I won, Daddy, I won!" exclaimed Lisa.

"Which cake would you like, Lisa?" asked Mrs. Stewart.

"I choose Miss Loomis's cake, ma'am," said Lisa happily.

"Yucky," said Will.

"Double yucky," said David.

"I'm sorry, Lisa," said Mrs. Stewart. "You will have to choose a different cake."

"Has Miss Loomis's cake already been chosen?" asked Lisa.

"No, honey," said Mrs. Stewart, "Miss Loomis's cake has been disqualified."

"Ha, ha," said Will.

Lisa began to get an uneasy feeling. Her father walked over to Mrs. Stewart.

"What seems to be the problem, Carol?" Mr. Parker asked.

"Lisa just needs to select another cake because the Loomis cake has been disqualified," said Mrs. Stewart.

"Disqualified—what are you really saying, Carol?" asked Mr. Parker.

"I'm saying that the Loomis cake might violate the health code," said Mrs. Stewart.

"And how could her cake possibly violate the health code?" asked Mr. Parker.

Tears began to well up in Lisa's eyes as a small crowd gathered in front of Mrs. Stewart.

"I'm saying that the Loomis cake may have been baked under unsanitary conditions," said Mrs. Stewart.

"Nasty," said Will.

"This is nothing but ignorance—pure ignorance," said Mr. Parker.

"I'm saying that because the Loomis cake was baked in the quarter, the kitchen could have been unsanitary," said Mrs. Stewart.

"You tell him, Carol; we don't want her dirty cake," said Betty Brown.

"Dirty cake, dirty cake," said David.

Lisa began to cry and buried her head in her father's suit. Mr. Parker held his daughter close.

"Do you still have Miss Loomis's cake?" asked Mr. Parker.

"It's in the back," said Mrs. Stewart. "If you want it that much, you can have it, you colored cuddler."

Mr. Parker ignored Mrs. Stewart's comment and turned to Lisa.

"Come on, Lisa," said Mr. Parker. "Let's go get your cake—your beautiful cake."

Mr. Parker took Lisa's trembling hand in his, and they walked through the swinging doors to the kitchen. There in the corner on a step stool next to the brooms and mops stood Miss Loomis's cake. It was a three-layer devil's food cake covered in white icing. The dark chocolate cake was visible through the white icing. Candy corn and candy pumpkins encircled the cake.

"It's beautiful, Daddy," said Lisa, regaining her composure.

"Yes, it is, Sissy," said Mr. Parker. "I'm so proud of you—you did a brave thing tonight."

"Thanks, Daddy, but you were braver," said Lisa. "Daddy, what's a colored cuddler?"

"Well, prejudiced people like to say the phrase 'colored cuddler' to feel superior to not only colored people but also white people who respect colored people. But this phrase cannot hurt us, Lisa, because we know the truth—white people are not better than colored people."

"That's right, Daddy," said Lisa with a shaky smile.

"Let's get out of here and go do something fun," said Mr. Parker.

Lisa dried her eyes and smiled.

"I want to go to the haunted house—Mrs. Cartwright is the mummy," said Lisa.

"Lead the way, Sissy," said Mr. Parker as he proudly carried Miss Loomis's cake past Mrs. Stewart and out of the lunchroom.

Lisa led her father to the school library, which had been transformed into a haunted house. The library door had been covered in brown construction paper, and plastic spiders and bats were hanging from the doorway. Inside, the room was dimly lit with green lights. Three spooky stations awaited visitors, with each station manned by parents dressed up as the mummy, Dracula, and Frankenstein.

"May I have a ticket, please?" Lisa asked her father.

Mr. Parker set the cake down and got a ticket from his pocket.

"Here you are," said Mr. Parker. "Don't get too scared."

"I won't, Daddy," said Lisa. "See you soon."

Lisa handed her ticket to Mrs. Powell and entered the haunted house. A large plastic spider dropped down from the ceiling onto Lisa. She screamed. Lisa had trouble seeing what was in front of her until she saw the mummy costume and smiled.

"Hi, Mrs. Cartwright," said Lisa. "This is Lisa."

"Hi, Lisa—I mean, Wendy. How do you like my costume? Pretty nifty, huh?" said Mrs. Cartwright, who was swaddled in white rags to look like an Egyptian mummy.

"Your costume is great," said Lisa.

"Well, the mummy commands you to reach your hand into this box of bats and find the token," said Mrs. Cartwright.

Lisa timidly stuck her right hand into a box of feathers. At the bottom of the box was a plastic whistle. Lisa pulled the whistle out of the box and handed it to Mrs. Cartwright.

"Very good, Lisa," said Mrs. Cartwright. "The mummy now commands you to reach into this box of snakes and find the token."

Lisa stuck her left hand into a box of rubber bands. At the bottom of the box was a button. Lisa pulled the button out of the box and handed it to Mrs. Cartwright.

"Very good, Lisa," said Mrs. Cartwright. "The mummy now commands you to reach into this box of bones and find the token."

Lisa stuck her right hand into a box of plastic tubes. At the bottom of the box was a penny. Lisa pulled the penny from the box and handed it to Mrs. Cartwright, who gave Lisa three pieces of candy.

"Why, I'd recognize those boxes anywhere—they are from the Green Ghost game," said Lisa.

"That's right," said Mrs. Cartwright. "Now take five steps forward, and you will meet Count Dracula!"

Lisa walked five steps in a forward direction, but instead of meeting Count Dracula, Lisa met Will and David in their ghost costumes. Only something was different about their costumes. Very different. In the green light a luminous cross appeared on the front of each costume. The crosses extended from the boys' shoulders to their feet. Lisa knew what this meant. Will and David weren't really ghosts. They were dressed up as members of the Ku Klux Klan, who burned huge crosses in front of Negroes' houses to scare them.

The boys began to taunt Lisa.

"We're gonna get Miss Loomis; we're gonna get Miss Loomis," they both whispered in singsongy voices.

Lisa started to cry, and the boys ran out of the haunted house.

Lisa was at another crossroads. If she did nothing, then Will and David might hurt Miss Loomis. If she told her father about Will and David's threats against Miss Loomis, then Will and David might hurt her tomorrow on the playground. Lisa summoned her courage.

"I've got to save Miss Loomis," she thought.

Lisa decided to leave the haunted house at once, but she had great difficulty retracing her steps in the green light. When she saw Mrs. Cartwright, she knew she was near the entrance.

"Lisa, you're going the wrong way," said Mrs. Cartwright.

"No, ma'am, I need to leave now," said Lisa.

"Is everything all right?" asked Mrs. Cartwright.

"I'm fine—it's just a little too scary for me," said Lisa.

Mrs. Cartwright escorted Lisa to the library door and out of the haunted house.

"Thank you," said Lisa.

"You're welcome," said Mrs. Cartwright.

Lisa looked around for her father. Mr. Parker was sitting in a chair with Miss Loomis's cake in his lap.

"Hi, Sissy," said Mr. Parker. "What's the matter?"

For the first time in her life Lisa had the courage to tell her father about Will and David.

"Will and David are dressed up like members of the Ku Klux Klan, and they may be after Miss Loomis," said Lisa.

"We need to get to her room immediately," said Mr. Parker.

"Follow me," said Lisa.

Lisa and her father walked down the corridor and up the stairs to the second floor. Miss Loomis occupied the room that was farthest from the stairs.

"Come on, Daddy," said Lisa, "her room is down here."

Lisa led the way down the main second-floor corridor. Mr. Parker walked more slowly than Lisa because he was carrying Miss Loomis's cake. They passed all of Lisa's other classrooms, which were filled with students and their parents.

As the two approached Miss Loomis's classroom, Lisa noticed something immediately.

"Daddy, something's wrong," said Lisa, "the lights are off."

"Wait for me," said Mr. Parker.

Lisa stopped at the door to Miss Loomis's classroom and peeked through a window. In the dark she saw the two fluorescent crosses on the costumes of Will and David. She could not see Miss Loomis.

"Daddy, hurry," called Lisa. "Will and David are inside."

"I'm almost there," said Mr. Parker. "Remain outside."

"Yes, sir," said Lisa. "And Daddy, I don't see Miss Loomis."

Lisa could hear voices coming from inside the room. The voices of Will and David.

"We're here to run you out of town, spook," said Will.

"You coon, you need to leave this school soon," said David.

"Why, we might have to burn a cross in your front yard," threatened Will.

Mr. Parker joined Lisa at the door to Miss Loomis's classroom. He could see the two large fluorescent crosses painted on Will and David's ghost costumes.

"Stay outside with the cake," said Mr. Parker as he placed the cake on a desk outside the classroom door.

Mr. Parker opened the door, walked inside, and turned on the light. He saw Will and David parading in front of Miss Loomis's desk. Crouched behind her desk was Miss Loomis. She was crying.

"Will and David," said Mr. Parker, "get out of here immediately, and if you ever bother Miss Loomis again, I will personally see to it that you are expelled from Wyatt."

Will and David stomped out of the classroom. Then they saw Lisa and the cake. They also saw that Mr. Parker was preoccupied with Miss Loomis. So the boys took a chance.

"Well, if it isn't Miss Smushed Nose," said Will. "You

may be wearing a pretty mask, but you are ugly on the inside."

Lisa began to tremble. She saw her father comforting Miss Loomis inside the classroom. She felt trapped. She was scared. Too scared to scream.

"Why, what if something happened to this cake?" said David.

"Please don't hurt the cake," pleaded Lisa.

"Don't worry," said Will, "that cake has Negro cooties, and we would never touch it."

"Yeah, I'll bet you will turn into a Negro if you eat it," said David.

"C'mon, David," said Will, "let's get out of here—we've had enough fun for one night."

Lisa watched the two boys run down the corridor and away from her. She was safe. She walked into Miss Loomis's classroom.

Miss Loomis was talking to her father. She was wearing a black shirtwaist dress with a pumpkin pin on the lapel. In front of her desk was a long table decorated with a Halloween tablecloth. On the table was a large crystal plate filled with chocolate cupcakes decorated with orange icing. The plate was full. Next to the cupcakes was a sheet of paper for the parents to sign. The sheet was blank.

Lisa saw her father give something to Miss Loomis.

"Here is my card," said Mr. Parker. "Call me if these boys give you any more trouble, and I will take care of everything. I encourage you not to quit—why, what would my Lisa do without you?"

"Hi, Daddy. Hi, Miss Loomis," said Lisa tentatively. "Is everything all right now?"

"Everything's fine now," said Mr. Parker, smiling. "Why, Miss Loomis has just been telling me what a good student you are."

"That's right, Lisa," said Miss Loomis shakily, "you are my shining star."

"Guess what, Miss Loomis," said Lisa. "I won your cake in the cakewalk."

"I am honored," said Miss Loomis.

"So are we," said Mr. Parker, glancing at his watch.

"We've got to go," said Mr. Parker. "It's time to meet your mother and the boys."

"Please sign the parents' sheet," said Miss Loomis. "I have to turn it in to the principal's office."

Mr. Parker looked down at the blank sheet of paper and shook his head.

"Where are the other signatures?" asked Mr. Parker while signing the sheet.

"Why, you were the only parent to visit my classroom," said Miss Loomis.

"Well, they don't know what they're missing," said Mr. Parker. "Ignorance, pure ignorance."

Lisa and Mr. Parker left Miss Loomis safe and sound. She would not be haunted by any more ghosts that night. Lisa and Mr. Parker, who was carrying Miss Loomis's cake, went back downstairs, where they met Mrs. Parker, Harold, and Mark. Mrs. Parker was holding the blue ribbon so that everyone could see.

"A cake," said Harold, "Sissy won a cake!"

"It's Miss Loomis's cake," said Lisa proudly.

"I would have chosen Mrs. Duke's cake—it's German chocolate," said Mrs. Parker.

"Penelope, don't get started," said Mr. Parker.

"Whatever you say, dear," said Mrs. Parker while smiling at Lisa.

"Boys," said Mr. Parker, "I sure am glad that you are friendly ghosts—I've had enough of mean ghosts to last a lifetime. Let's all go home and have a piece of Miss Loomis's cake."

"Ozella, too?" asked Lisa.

"Ozella, too," said Mr. Parker.

Reverend Reed was waiting in his car for Miss Loomis. She finally arrived carrying all of the Halloween cupcakes from her open house. She was crying.

"I want to quit," cried Miss Loomis. "I can't take it anymore."

"What happened?" asked Reverend Reed.

"The two mean boys, Will and David, dressed up like Klan members," said Miss Loomis. "They said hateful words and told me to quit teaching at Wyatt."

"Calm down, Annie," said Reverend Reed. "Now, how do you know that the boys weren't really dressed up as ghosts?"

"Because their white costumes had glow-in-the-dark crosses painted on them," said Miss Loomis. "And Will threatened to burn a cross in my front yard."

"Did the boys lay a hand on you?" asked Reverend Reed.

"No," said Miss Loomis, "but they scared me to death with their words."

"Pay attention to the Scripture, Sister," said Reverend Reed, "and turn the other cheek to these boys. Besides, if you quit, then these white boys win. Now, you don't want that, Annie."

"I will turn the other cheek," said Miss Loomis, "but Principal Breen could force me to quit due to the low attendance at my open house."

"You let me handle Principal Breen," said Reverend Reed. "You just focus on your classes, and everything will work out for the best."

"Yes, sir," said Miss Loomis.

Reverend Reed noticed that Miss Loomis was still trembling.

"How about I get one of the church elders to sit in his car in front of your house tonight?" asked Reverend Reed.

"I would like that," said Miss Loomis. "I'm so scared that I can't stop shaking."

"Well, you can calm your fears," said Reverend Reed, "because no one is going to hurt you. You have God on your side."

"I know that's right," said Miss Loomis.

A full moon held vigil over the houses of Miss Loomis and Lisa. The moon made no distinction between the parts of town in which they lived. Its beams shone on white or Negro, rich or poor alike. The moon held no prejudice.

That night Lisa dreamed of Miss Loomis. She dreamed that Miss Loomis gave Dr. King's "I Have a Dream" speech before thousands at the Lincoln Memorial. Dr. King stood on the sideline and clapped. Lisa then dreamed that Miss Loomis turned into a pumpkin that Will and David began to carve.

Chapter Thirteen

The Corn King

Halloween may have been over, but there was still excitement in the air. The Big Bear grocery store in the Parkers' neighborhood was hosting a celebrity—the Corn King.

The Corn King was one of the tallest men in the world. He stood almost eight feet tall in his bare feet. When he wore his crown, he was over eight feet tall.

The Corn King was not really a king. He was the official sponsor of the Corn King Margarine Company, which gave him the title of Corn King because this company used corn oil in its margarine.

Whenever the Corn King appeared at a grocery store, the store would run a special on its Corn King margarine. If a customer bought a package of Corn King margarine, the Corn King would give the customer an autographed photograph of himself.

The Corn King was really just Howard Small from Dayton, Ohio, who just happened to be considered a giant in height. Mr. Small began his career as "the Tall Small" in freak shows at carnivals. He soon grew to be the star attraction at carnivals. When his carnival act was in Indianapolis, an executive with the Indy Margarine Company saw "the Tall Small" and asked him if he would like to be the official sponsor of his company. When Small accepted this offer, the name "Corn King" was born. Small graduated from being just a sideshow act at small-time carnivals to the star of national commercials.

A king was born. So when the Corn King was slated to appear at the Big Bear grocery store in Montgomery, Alabama, on November 20, 1968, it was a big deal. Everyone wanted to see the Corn King—everyone, that is, except Lisa.

To Lisa, the appearance of the Corn King was like the freak show all over again.

"First the bearded lady, then the Corn King," thought Lisa. "What will be next, the harelip?"

Lisa was determined not to go see the Corn King. But try as she might, she was fated to gaze upon this autumnal giant.

"Lisa, you simply must go," said Mrs. Parker. "Why, everyone will be there."

"But I can take care of baby Elizabeth while you take the boys," said Lisa.

The boys were dying to see the Corn King. They thought he was a real king like Old King Cole. They also thought he was a giant that lived in the sky atop a beanstalk.

"Ozella will take care of Elizabeth," said Mrs. Parker. "Besides, I need you to help me with the boys—the crowd could be enormous."

"Yes, ma'am," said Lisa.

On the appointed day, Lisa, Harold, and Mark piled into their mother's car for the short ride to the grocery store. Lisa was holding a Polaroid camera to take pictures of the boys with the Corn King. Harold and Mark were wearing play crowns and holding plastic swords.

"And don't cut his head off in the pictures," laughed Mrs. Parker. "Why, he may be too tall to photograph."

"Yes, ma'am," said Lisa. "I'll do my best."

The parking lot outside the grocery store was packed with cars. There was a line of people extending from the store onto the sidewalk outside.

"I knew we should have gotten here earlier," fussed Mrs. Parker. "Thank goodness this car is small enough to squeeze into this space."

Mrs. Parker inched her car into a small space in front of the grocery store. Mrs. Parker then used her social skills with the store manager to get to the front of the line.

"Excuse me, Mr. Bailey," whispered Mrs. Parker. "I'll buy a side of beef from you if you let me and my children move to the front of the line."

Never one to pass up a sale, particularly one as profitable as this, Mr. Bailey ushered Mrs. Parker, Lisa, Harold, and Mark to the front of the line.

"Excuse me, but I was first," said an unknown woman.

"Pardon me, but regular customers go first," said Mr. Bailey.

While the boys engaged in a mock sword fight, Mrs. Parker began waving to all of her friends and neighbors who were now behind her in line. Some waved back; others paid her no attention. Lisa was humiliated—she'd cut in line in front of all of her friends.

"Great," thought Lisa, "everyone is probably mad at me."

Lisa then looked back to see Cathy waving to her and smiling. Lisa waved and smiled back.

Lisa looked around the store. Big Bear had gone all out for the Corn King. In the back of the store in front of the frozen foods was a banner advertising Corn King margarine along with a special free-standing refrigerated compartment filled with Corn King margarine. On the banner was a picture of the Corn King.

Lisa then heard a trumpet fanfare over the grocery store loudspeaker. The music heralded the entrance of the Corn King from his seat next to the rotten vegetables in the back of the store. In walked an extremely tall, very thin man. He was wearing a regal robe made of red velveteen trimmed in fake white fur. On his head sat a large gold crown with a red velveteen top. His pants were extremely high-waisted, and his cuffs were much too short.

The Corn King walked in front of the frozen-food section until he came to the center of his banner. When he stood erect, his crown became entangled in the banner. Despite his best efforts, the more he tried to untangle himself, the more tangled he became. Mr. Bailey dispatched the butcher and greengrocer to the scene to untangle the king. These two succeeded in removing the Corn King's crown, which caused the banner to fall to the ground. The Corn King was effectively dethroned in front of the crowd.

"Mama, he's not a king anymore," cried Harold.

"Not king," cried Mark.

"Now, children," said Mrs. Parker, "he will get his crown back any moment."

And any moment it might be. Mr. Bailey had now interceded in the matter, and he was using scissors to extricate the crown from the banner. The scissors cut the picture of the Corn King into small pieces while freeing the crown. The Corn King knelt, and Mr. Bailey then placed the crown back on the Corn King's head. The Corn King stood back up while the crowd applauded.

The Corn King did not speak but signaled for the Parkers to come forward. Mrs. Parker pushed Lisa, Harold, and Mark in front of the Corn King.

"Lisa," yelled Mrs. Parker, "get a picture of the boys with the Corn King."

"Yes, ma'am," said Lisa.

Lisa knelt down and tried to get the faces of the boys and the Corn King in the camera's viewfinder. When she was unable to frame the picture, she backed up, but to no avail.

"It's no use," said Lisa. "I can't get the boys in the picture without cutting the Corn King's head off."

"Maybe I can help," said a tiny voice.

Lisa looked up to see the Corn King kneeling between the boys for a picture. Lisa looked in the viewfinder and snapped the picture. Then Harold and Mark began touching the Corn King.

"He doesn't feel like a giant to me," said Harold.

"Not giant," said Mark.

"He's really skinny," said Harold.

"Kinny," said Mark.

"Please excuse my brothers," said Lisa. "We enjoyed meeting you."

The Corn King then gave autographed photographs of himself to Lisa, Harold, and Mark (and Mrs. Parker).

"Let's go, children," Mrs. Parker said.

Lisa held hands with Harold and Mark as they walked to their mother's car. On the ride home, Harold was filled with questions.

"Is the Corn King related to Katie?" asked Harold.

"No," said Mrs. Parker. "Why would you ask that?"

"One is too tall, and one is too short," said Harold.

"The Corn King is a giant, and Katie is a midget," said Mrs. Parker. "They are not related."

"Why is the Corn King a giant?" asked Harold.

"God made him that way," said Mrs. Parker.

"Why is Katie a midget?" asked Harold.

"God made her that way," said Mrs. Parker.

"Why?" asked Harold.

"Because," said Mrs. Parker.

Lisa listened to her brother's questions and wondered why God made her the way she was. Because.

Chapter Fourteen

The Pageant

December ushered in the first winter weather of the year. The sixth-grade Christmas pageant was just two weeks away, but Lisa had her mind on other things—Mark's third birthday. This year Mark was having his party at the Parker house. The theme for the party was cowboys and Indians. Lisa and Cathy would be in charge of arts and crafts—the youngsters would be making sheriffs' badges and Indian headbands out of construction paper, pipe cleaners, and glitter.

Mrs. Parker got Mark's birthday cake from Liger's Bakery—it was a chocolate sheet cake with white icing and plastic cowboys and Indians on horseback. The birthday party began with a game of Pin the Tail on the Donkey. Mark pinned his tail on the donkey's nose. Lisa touched her nose and winced. Harold won the game by pinning his tail closest to the donkey's rear end.

"I won, Brother, I won," said Harold.

"Good, Bubba, I so gwad," said Mark.

A game of Hi Ho! Cherry-o followed. Mark's friend Anderson won by having the most plastic cherries in his bucket. Then it was on to arts and crafts.

"Can everyone decorate your sheriff's badge with glitter?" asked Cathy. "First put some glue on your badge, sprinkle glitter on top, and then shake it."

"Wike this," said Mark as he shook the excess glitter from his badge.

"That's great, Mark," said Cathy, who was busy stapling pipe cleaners to the center of the paper feathers.

"Can everyone glue the paper feathers to your headbands?" asked Lisa. "First, get your brown strip of construction paper, then place dots of glue on the paper, then press your paper feathers to the glue."

The children began gluing paper feathers to their strips of construction paper.

"When you are finished, I will measure your head and staple your headband in place," said Lisa. "I will also give your feathers more support by stapling them to your headbands."

When the gluing and stapling were over, four boys and three girls were wearing sheriffs' badges and Indian headbands.

"I want to make a headband for Ozella," said Harold.

"Why?" said Mrs. Parker.

"Because Ozella is an Indian," said Harold.

"No, she's not," said Lisa.

"Well, Ozella has brown skin like Indians," said Harold.

"No," said Lisa, "Ozella is a Negro, not an Indian, and her skin is darker that an Indian's skin."

"No more of that talk," said Mrs. Parker.

"What is Negro?" asked Harold.

"Now see what you've started?" said Mrs. Parker. "Harold, stop asking questions."

"Negro is a group of people with dark skin who used to live in Africa with lions and tigers," said Lisa. "Isn't that right, Ozella?"

"I believe so, sweetie pie," said Ozella.

"I want to be Negro and live with lions and tigers," said Harold.

"Harold, if you don't hush, I'm going to wash your mouth out with soap," said Mrs. Parker.

"If you lived in Africa, Sissy would miss you," said Lisa.

"I won't really go to Africa," said Harold.

"Don't go, Bubba," said Mark.

"Time to play Simon Says," said Lisa.

"Come on, children," said Cathy.

After games came cake and ice cream and the opening of presents. Then it was time for the guests to go home, with party favors in tow.

"Cathy, thank you so much for helping with Mark's birthday party," said Mrs. Parker.

"You're welcome, Mrs. Parker," said Cathy.

"Are you busy getting ready for the Christmas pageant?" asked Mrs. Parker.

"Yes, ma'am," said Cathy. "Lisa and I are on the decorating committee, and we are trying to turn the stage into a winter wonderland."

"Wonderful," said Mrs. Parker.

"See you on Monday, Cath," said Lisa, who walked Cathy to her mother's car. "That's the day of the big announcement."

"I know," said Cathy. "The principal will announce the Christmas queen and her court," Cathy explained to her mother. "I'm keeping my fingers crossed that we make the cut."

"Me, too," said Lisa. "Bye-bye."

Lisa walked back into her house to eat lunch. Her mother was waiting for her in the kitchen.

"Sissy," said Mrs. Parker, "I have a surprise for you in my bedroom."

"Really?" said Lisa while following her mother to her parents' bedroom.

There on the king-sized bed lay the most beautiful dress that Lisa had ever seen. It was an emerald green sequined formal in her size.

"Don't you just love it?" said Mrs. Parker. "Why, you'll make the most beautiful queen in Wyatt history."

"But Mother," said Lisa, "I don't know if I will be the queen."

"Sure you will," said Mrs. Parker. "Why, you're the best student in the whole grade. Try the dress on, right now."

To Lisa, the queen had to have good grades and be pretty. Lisa wasn't sure she was pretty enough to be queen. She felt assured of a place in the queen's court due to her good grades. The pressure was on. Lisa had to be queen to please her mother. Suddenly, the emerald green dress didn't look so pretty.

With her mother's help, Lisa put on the formal gown. It fit perfectly, and her padded bra accentuated the bust line. Lisa felt like a princess standing in front of the full-length mirror.

"I had this gown custom-made for you," said Mrs. Parker. "I will take you shoe shopping next week. And for the finishing touch, I am letting you wear my pearl necklace with the gown."

"Thanks, Mom," said Lisa, "but remember, the principal doesn't announce the queen and her court until Monday."

"I'm not worried," said Mrs. Parker.

But worried Lisa was. She could barely sleep or eat for the next two days. On Sunday, Lisa wasn't feeling very pretty. All she could do was look at her formal gown and pray that she would be the queen.

The big day arrived, and Lisa wore her lucky dress to school. The dress was a lime green culotte dress with white polka dots. She wore her white go-go boots for extra luck. The announcement was made over the loudspeaker during homeroom with Mrs. Duke.

"May I have you attention, please," said Mr. Breen. "The Christmas queen is Cathy Cartwright. The members of her court are Becky Owens, Roxanne Phillips, and Sallie Trotter."

Lisa was devastated. Not only did she not make queen—she didn't even make a member of the queen's court. Thanks to her mother, she had a formal gown and nowhere to wear it. Thanks to her nose and scars, she had an ugly face and nowhere to wear it. At the core of her being, Lisa truly felt ugly for the first time. She also understood the bitter truth that some people believe that physical appearance is more important than anything else, even good grades.

Lisa congratulated Cathy for being queen and tried to make it through the rest of the day. Even Miss Loomis's class didn't cheer her up. And things would be even worse when she got home.

After being picked up from school, Lisa sat quietly in the back. Mrs. Parker pulled the car into the driveway, and she and the children went inside their home.

"Well, tell me the good news," said Mrs. Parker.

Lisa burst into tears. "I didn't make it," she cried. "I didn't even get in the court."

"I don't believe it," said Mrs. Parker. "Who made it?"

"Cathy is queen, and Becky, Roxanne, and Sallie are in the court," said Lisa.

"I am furious," said Mrs. Parker. "You are smarter than all of those girls put together."

"But I'm not pretty, Mom," cried Lisa.

"Don't ever say that," yelled Mrs. Parker. "You are beautiful in your own way."

"I'm sorry you went to all that expense for nothing," cried Lisa.

"Nonsense," said Mrs. Parker. "Why, you'll get to wear that dress on other occasions."

Mrs. Parker began to pace back and forth like a tiger in a cage. She was thinking.

"Of course," said Mrs. Parker. "I know why you didn't make the cut—it's all your father's fault!"

"What do you mean?" asked Lisa.

"Your father represents Negroes," said Mrs. Parker. "And the selection committee obviously thinks that is wrong, and they blackballed you from the pageant."

"That's not true, Mother," said Lisa. "I didn't make the cut because of the cut on my lip, not Daddy's clients."

"You're naive, Lisa," said Mrs. Parker. "The Negro question controls everything."

"What do you mean?" asked Lisa.

"I mean that white folks who help Negroes can lose their businesses and their homes," said Mrs. Parker. "Why, your father's law practice has lost business since your father started representing Negroes."

Mr. Parker walked into the room.

"What did you say about my law practice?" asked Mr. Parker.

"Nothing, dear," said Mrs. Parker. "Poor Sissy—she didn't make it as Christmas queen or a member of the court."

"I'm so sorry, Sissy," said Mr. Parker. "You'll always be queen of my heart."

"Thank you, Daddy," said Lisa. "Mama says I lost out because you represent Negroes."

"Well, your mama could be right," said Mr. Parker. "And if it's my fault that you lost, then I apologize. I don't know why the selection committee voted the way it did, but I can tell you one thing. If I had been on that committee, you would have gotten my vote as the smartest and prettiest girl in the sixth grade."

"Thank you, Daddy," said Lisa, smiling.

The day of the pageant came and went, but to Lisa the feeling of being ugly persisted long past the sequins and the pearls.

Chapter Fifteen

The Nose

The teasing of Will and David paled in comparison to a teacher's rude question. It all began during a January day in fifth period. It was too cold to have P.E. outside, so Mrs. Cook decided to entertain the students inside.

This seventy-year-old teacher had played so much tennis that she had a year-round tan. She looked like a wrinkled sultana raisin. Tennis she may have mastered, but Wyatt didn't have a tennis court.

Mrs. Cook, unfortunately, knew nothing about the sports played in sixth grade. She failed to allow the sixth grade to participate in the Montgomery Track and Field Games, and Wyatt was always in last place by default, a constant embarrassment to the school.

Yet Mrs. Cook was always in first place among the teachers at Wyatt because her brother was on the school board.

So on that winter's day, Mrs. Cook commandeered the sixth grade science room for a talk.

"Attention, class," yelled Mrs. Cook. She blew her whistle and said, "Please sit down."

The students sat in random desks. Mrs. Cook often

had these talks to reminisce about her short-lived tennis career and to play mental tennis matches with her students.

"Boring," thought Lisa.

But this talk was different. This talk was about faces.

"Class," Mrs. Cook asked, "if you could ask fifty people to change one thing about their faces, what would most of these people say?"

Lisa swallowed hard. Tears began to well up in her eyes, and her nervous stomach surfaced.

"Is she talking about my nose?" wondered Lisa.

"Let's have a show of hands for eyes," Mrs. Cook said.

Only Clara Martin raised her hand.

"Let's have a show of hands for ears," Mrs. Cook said.

Only four hands rose in the air.

Mrs. Cook then went through the other parts of the face, saving the nose for last.

"How many noses have we?" Mrs. Cook asked.

Mrs. Cook counted and reported that the nose had won.

"Do you know why the nose won?" declared Mrs. Cook, "Do you? Because more people are unhappy with the look of their noses than they are with any other part of their faces. Why, the nose can be too long, too upturned, or too flattened."

The class was staring at Lisa—staring at Lisa's nose. Lisa laid her head on her desk to hide her nose and began to cry.

"No crying in my class," barked Mrs. Cook. "Just suck

it up, you crybaby. Why, you'd never make it through a tennis match!"

Lisa tried to dry her tears, but she couldn't stop crying.

"Crybabies have to stand in front of the class and suck their thumbs. Come on up here, Lisa," Mrs. Cook demanded.

Lisa had never been so humiliated in her life. She stood up while still crying and walked to the front of the classroom.

"Put your thumb in your mouth, crybaby," Mrs. Cook ordered.

Lisa reluctantly placed her right thumb in her mouth. She was crying even harder now.

"All right, Lisa," Mrs. Cook barked. "We are playing a tennis match, and I'm up forty–love. I'm serving for the match. What are you going to do, Lisa?"

Lisa stopped crying, took her thumb out of her mouth, and thought. She remembered the tennis her father had taught her. And then something happened way down deep inside of Lisa. She found her courage. The courage to stand up to Mrs. Cook.

"Lisa, what are you going to do?" repeated Mrs. Cook.

"Nothing," replied Lisa. "You just double-faulted."

The class laughed, and Mrs. Cook frowned.

"OK, the score is now forty–fifteen, Lisa," Mrs. Cook said. "What happens now?"

"You serve, and I return it down the line for a winner," says Lisa. "The score is now forty–thirty."

"I now serve an ace and win the match," says Mrs. Cook. "As I always say, crybabies never win."

"But winners sometimes cry," says Lisa. "Therefore, winners can be crybabies, too."

"But you will always be a loser because of your flattened nose," said Mrs. Cook.

"People who make fun of the way other people look are the biggest losers of all," said Lisa. "Game, set, match."

As Lisa walked back to her desk, she noticed that many of her classmates were smiling at her. Lisa learned that day that a nose is not just a nose. And a teacher is not just a teacher.

Lisa awoke to the same anxious feelings and nervous stomach she had on any other school day. Yet something was different this morning. Lisa remembered her courage, and some of her anxious thoughts went away. Lisa put on her school clothes as if she were preparing for battle. Her gold sweater and pleated gold miniskirt became the tunic of a Roman warrior. Her gold kneesocks and brown leather loafers became the leather sandals of a Roman warrior. And her navy peacoat became the breastplate and shield of a Roman warrior.

"If I have the courage to stand up to Mrs. Cook," thought Lisa, "then I have the courage to stand up to the mean boys."

Lisa remained strong during homeroom and the first two classes. Yet when it was time to go outside for recess, Lisa began to get scared. Her navy peacoat no longer felt like the breastplate and shield of a Roman warrior. It was just a coat, and a flimsy one at that. When Lisa went outside, Will and David were waiting for her.

"Well, if it isn't Miss Nosy," said Will. "Lose any more tennis matches?"

"You're just a big loser, Miss Flattened Nose," said David.

Lisa began to breathe hard, and a wave of nausea overcame her. She looked around for help, but she saw no one who would help her. Mrs. Duke occupied her usual spot on a far-off bench talking to another teacher. Lisa had two choices. She could do nothing and remain scared, or she could summon her courage and stand up to the bullies. Lisa began to replace her feelings of self-doubt with feelings of self-confidence. Her courage returned, and she decided to confront the bullies.

Lisa repeated her mantra from the day before.

"People who make fun of the way other people look are the biggest losers of all," said Lisa.

"Are you calling me a loser?" asked Will.

Lisa swallowed hard. The scary feelings were returning.

"Yes," said Lisa timidly.

"Why, you little runt," said Will. "See how you like this."

Will ran up to Lisa and pushed her from behind. Lisa fell forward into the dirt with her palms bracing her fall. A rock tore a gash in her left knee, and blood began trickling down her leg onto her kneesock. Cathy ran over to Lisa and helped her to her feet.

"If you tell," said Will, "I will hurt you even more next time."

"I won't tell," cried Lisa.

Lisa's courage was gone, and in its place was pure fear.

When recess was over, Lisa tried to hide her bloody knee from Mrs. Duke to no avail.

"Lisa, what happened to your knee?" asked Mrs. Duke.

"I accidentally tripped and fell on a rock," said Lisa.

Lisa had just lied to Mrs. Duke. Lisa knew that it was wrong to lie, but this lie protected her from the bullies.

"Besides," reasoned Lisa to herself, "I told a half-truth—I did fall on a rock. I just didn't accidentally trip—Will intentionally pushed me to the ground. But Mrs. Duke doesn't need to know about Will—that will be my scary secret."

Lisa's lie served as a shield of double protection—it protected Will from getting into trouble, and it also protected Lisa from getting hurt by Will.

"Well, go in the bathroom and clean yourself up," said Mrs. Duke.

"Yes, ma'am," said Lisa.

Lisa limped to the girls' bathroom and began sobbing uncontrollably. Her tears mixed with the dried blood on her knee, causing the wound to burn. She wet a paper towel and began wiping the blood from her knee. Yet she could not wipe the lie that she had told Mrs. Duke from her mind. That lie would be a constant reminder of the bullies and the time her courage failed her.

The playground became the "hateground" to Lisa. Will and David hated her, and she began to hate them. Lisa also began to feel sorry for herself. And a bad seed was sown.

"Why is everybody always picking on me?" thought

Lisa. "Why, it's time I started picking on somebody else. Then the bullies will start teasing that person and leave me alone."

And that "somebody else" took the form of Clara Martin. Like Lisa, Clara also had a physical disability. Unlike Lisa, Clara was able to hide her disability and avoid teasing from the bullies.

"It's time for Clara to pay the price for her weak eyes," thought Lisa vindictively.

Clara Martin was a homely looking girl. Everything about her was plain. She wore plain dresses and shoes. She had plain mousy brown hair that was always parted on the side and held in place with a plain brown barrette. All of her features were plain with one notable exception. Clara Martin had unusual eyes. Her eyes were too small for the rest of her face.

The reason Clara's eyes were too small was because Clara was born that way. Her eyes were green, and they slanted toward her nose not unlike the eyes of someone from Asia. Her eyes oozed yellow fluid, which formed crusty particles encircling her lids. Clara's vision was extremely poor, and she hid her unusual eyes behind very thick glasses.

Lisa knew of Clara's eyes because they were not unlike her own nose. Yet instead of feeling empathy for Clara, Lisa felt jealous of Clara because Clara wasn't bullied like she was. So Lisa decided to even the score by teasing Clara. The teasing began at recess the following day.

"Well, if it isn't Miss Four Eyes out for a stroll," Lisa yelled.

Will and David turned to look at Lisa as she pointed to Clara.

"How many fingers am I holding up, Clarabelle, or do you need stronger glasses?" asked Lisa.

Will and David began to laugh while Clara began to cry.

"Oh, look," yelled Lisa, "her eyes do work—she's crying real tears."

"Mind your own business, Miss Smushed Nose," yelled Clara.

Lisa was stunned. Clara was now teasing her. Lisa immediately put her hand over her nose.

"You can dish it out, but you can't take it, Miss Nosy," said Clara.

Lisa couldn't believe her eyes. Will and David had stopped laughing at Clara and were now laughing at her. Her plan had backfired. Now she had three classmates teasing her. Lisa had learned her lesson. She would not tease Clara anymore. But the damage had already been done. Clara no longer trusted Lisa. Lisa would have to regain Clara's trust.

In P.E. class later that day, Mrs. Cook let the students play dodgeball. Lisa dreaded this game, which Will and David called "Smushed Nose–ball" because Will and David always aimed the ball at Lisa's nose. A bloody nose sometimes resulted, but Lisa protected Will and David from blame by saying it was just an ordinary nosebleed. But on this day Will and David had more than one target.

Will was wielding a dodgeball in his beefy hands. Lisa was shaking like a leaf and running across the circle as fast as her legs would carry her. But Clara was unaware that Will had his sights set on her. She stood frozen in his headlights, blinking her slanted, thickly encrusted eyes in disbelief.

"Dodgeball is Lisa's enemy, not mine," Clara thought. Yet when Clara saw Will take aim at her glasses, she screamed in horror. Her poor vision dulled her reflexes, and the ball hit Clara squarely in the face, breaking her heavy glasses in twain and knocking Clara off her feet.

Lisa ran to Clara, picked up her cleft glasses, and helped her stand again.

"It's all right, Clara," Lisa said while wiping the grass and blood from her tear-stained face. "This is all my fault—I'm so sorry that I teased you."

"You didn't hurt me—Will did," said Clara.

"But I hurt your feelings, and that's just as bad," said Lisa.

Clara's injury gave Lisa even more courage that day on the playground.

"Why, it's two against one," Lisa yelled to Will.

Lisa then grabbed the dodgeball in her tiny, doll-like hands. She looked Will square in the eye, like David wielding his tiny slingshot at Goliath, and she threw that ball with Superman-like strength.

The throw caught Will off guard. He had been laughing at Lisa and Clara and didn't know what hit him. But hit him it did—right in the groin. He moaned in agony. Lisa screamed with delight and started jumping up and down.

Dumbstruck by what had just happened Clara looked

fuzzily at Will's painful wincing and then at Lisa's jumping. The dodgeball circle of hate began to collapse as the students, one by one, began to crowd around Clara and Lisa, each child clapping and smiling.

"You did it, Lisa," yelled Cathy with delight. "You finally hit him—he can't hurt you anymore."

A truce was reached between Lisa and Clara that day—a separate peace treaty signed by blood sisters. Sisters who shared scars that no one else could see—those horrible scars the size of football fields that destroyed a little bit of themselves each day. Lisa and Clara's bloody scars paled in comparison to their emotional scars, which hurt whenever the mean boys teased them.

Lisa escorted Clara to their next class, where Miss Loomis wiped the blood from Clara's face. Clara told Miss Loomis what Will did to her. The principal's office called Clara's mother, who said she would bring Clara another pair of glasses. The principal's office also called Will's parents, who said they would buy Clara a new pair of glasses.

Yet Clara didn't need her glasses on the playground that day. Clara and Lisa shared a "second" sight—all insight, foresight, and hindsight merged in a special vision. A "smushed" nose and encrusted eyes belied the black, gaping holes inside. Ordinary vision underlooked these dark recesses. Yet each time Clara and Lisa stood up to the bullies, the black, gaping holes began to shrink. Courage replaced fear. Two tiny voices, steadfast and true, could stand up to the bullies' threats. Teamwork strengthened resolve. Lisa would never sacrifice another student to the bullies' fiefdom. Strength lay in sisterhood, not solipsism.

Yes, Lisa and Clara were different from the others in their grade. Yet they didn't need to leap tall buildings in a single bound. They weren't faster than speeding bullets. They weren't stronger than locomotives.

Lisa and Clara didn't need Superman's X-ray vision. They were blind, but now they see.

Chapter Seventeen

The Valentine

A new girl joined Lisa's class in February. Her name was Karen Avery, and her father was fighting overseas in the Vietnamese War. Lisa frequently watched the war on television, and it made her sad to see the United States soldiers injured or killed in the war. Yet Lisa had never known an actual person related to a U.S. soldier in Vietnam until she met Karen.

Karen had bright red hair and freckles. She wore a silver ladybug locket around her neck. When Karen pulled back the ladybug's two wings, a photograph of Karen's father in his military uniform emerged. Karen wore this locket every day.

Karen was an only child and lived with her mother in Lisa's neighborhood. Although Karen's father was stationed at Montgomery's Maxwell Air Force Base, Karen's mother chose to live off base so that Karen could attend a Montgomery public school.

Lisa and Karen became fast friends. Lisa loved to hear stories of Karen's growing up near military bases all over the country, and Karen loved to hear stories of Lisa's growing up with two brothers and a sister. Lisa visited Karen during the first week in February, and

Karen visited Lisa during the second week in February. "Tell me the story of Harold and Trixie again, Lisa," said Karen. "I can't believe that dog was that big!"

"Trixie is a standard schnauzer, and she is almost as tall as a Shetland pony. Now you tell me the story of living in California, Karen," said Lisa. "Did you really go to school with Negroes?"

"People in California don't use the word 'Negro' anymore—they say 'black,'" said Karen. "Yes, there were three black students in my class in California—two girls and one boy. The girls were nice, but the boy was mean. He was always making fun of my white skin and my red hair and freckles."

"I know all about mean boys," said Lisa.

"You do?" asked Karen.

Lisa paused and took a deep breath. She began to get that sinking feeling in the pit of her stomach.

"If I tell Karen my secret and why Will and David are mean to me, then she might not like me anymore," thought Lisa. "I haven't even told Cathy my secret."

"What's wrong, Lisa?" asked Karen. "You know that I like you, no matter what."

Lisa looked deep inside and found her courage again. She would trust Karen with her secret.

"Karen," said Lisa, "I was born with a hole in the roof of my mouth and a hole in my upper lip."

"But you don't have those holes now," said Karen.

"I know. When I was a baby, I had two surgeries to close those holes. That's why my nose is flattened on one side and why I have scars from my nose to my lip."

"I can hardly tell, Lisa," said Karen. "I think that you look great."

"Thanks, Karen," said Lisa, "that means a lot to me."

"But what about the mean boys?" asked Karen.

"Will and David are the mean boys," said Lisa. "They make fun of my nose on the playground. They've been on their best behavior recently, but I'm sure you will see their true colors before long."

"Guess what, Lisa," said Karen.

"What?" asked Lisa apprehensively.

"Since you told me your secret, I like you even more!" exclaimed Karen.

Lisa grinned from ear to ear.

On the playground the next day, Karen saw the true colors of Will and David. It was a cold, wintry day, and Lisa and Karen were huddled together to keep warm. Will and David approached the girls.

"Well, if it isn't Miss Smushed Nose," said Will. "Is your new friend gonna protect you?"

"Yes, she is," said Karen.

"I'm not scared of you, Miss Red Head," said Will.

"Well, my father is a soldier, and he can make you behave," said Karen.

"Your father could be dead, for all you know," said Will.

"Yeah, dead," said David.

"You take that back," cried Karen. "My father is alive, and if he were here, he would skin you alive."

"Oh, I'm so scared," said Will in a baby voice. "For all you know your father could be a coward."

"Yeah, the Cowardly Lion," said David.

"Stop it," cried Lisa. "Karen's father is a hero."

"Yeah, a hero like that sissy Underdog," said Will.

"Leave Underdog out of this," said Lisa. "Will and David, you owe Karen an apology."

"No truce, no apology," said Will.

"No apology, no retreat," said Lisa.

The playground was becoming a battleground. A war was being waged between Lisa and Karen and Will and David. There were no soldiers to fight for either side—just four children as the harbingers of good and evil.

The playground war became the Civil War in Miss Newell's class. The class was studying Lincoln's birthday, and Miss Newell had a special reason to celebrate.

"Attention, class," said Miss Newell in her sweet voice. "I have a special assignment for you today."

"Oh, no," moaned Will.

"Now, now, my sweet, sweet children," cooed Miss Newell. "You will write a one-page essay on why the death of Abraham Lincoln was for the best."

"This sounds hard," said David.

"It won't be hard if you listen to me," yelled Miss Newell in her mean voice.

"Isn't it *President* Lincoln?" said Lisa.

"It's Abraham Lincoln in my class," said Miss Newell in her mean voice. "The man should never have been president."

"Honest Abe," said David.

"Not in my class," yelled mean Miss Newell.

The sweet Miss Newell now surfaced.

"Now, children, sweet, sweet children," purred Miss Newell. "It's so easy—Lincoln caused the Civil War, so his death reunited the country. As I've said before, every cloud has a silver lining."

"But President Lincoln did a great thing for this country," said Karen. "He freed the slaves."

"Now, now, the plantation life was a happy life," said Miss Newell sweetly.

"That's not true," said Karen.

"Well, it looks like we have another color-blind student in the class," said mean Miss Newell. "You're in fine company because Abraham Lincoln was as color-blind as a bat. Now do you see why his death was a good thing?"

Karen answered, "There's nothing wrong with my eyesight."

"Oh, yes there is, sugar," replied the sickeningly sweet Miss Newell. "You can't see the difference between your own skin color and a Negro's skin color. Why, you just love Negroes, you Yankee girl!"

Karen looked at Lisa in disbelief. Lisa raised her hand in the air.

"Miss Newell, may I write my essay on why the assassination of President Lincoln was for the worst?" Lisa asked.

"Me, too?" asked Karen.

"Do as you will," said mean Miss Newell. "And class, if you want to pass, not a word of this essay to your parents."

Another teacher secret. Lisa was about to burst. But keep this secret she did. Karen, however, did not.

"I'm going to tell my mother what she called me," whispered Karen.

"Don't do it, Karen," whispered Lisa. "Miss Newell may flunk you if you tell."

"Oh, she's just bluffing," whispered Karen.

"No, she's not," whispered Lisa. "Becky Owens told her mother about Miss Newell's mean voice, and she got a D on her next test."

"OK, well, I won't tell my mother, but I will tell Miss Loomis," whispered Karen. "Surely she can put a stop to this nonsense."

"Please keep Miss Loomis out of this," whispered Lisa.

"No," whispered Karen. "She is black, and she will help us."

The rest of the day limped along until it was time for Miss Loomis's class. Before class began, Karen approached Miss Loomis, who was seated at her desk. Karen told Miss Loomis everything that had happened in Miss Newell's class that day. Miss Loomis did not respond. Instead she looked down at her lesson plan and began to tremble.

"Don't you understand?" Karen said. "She called me color-blind."

Miss Loomis finally made eye contact with Karen.

"I understand," said Miss Loomis.

"Well, aren't you going to do something?" asked Karen.

"I have no control over Miss Newell or what she says in her class," said Miss Loomis.

"But you're black," said Karen. "Surely you can help."

"I am one colored teacher in an all-white school," said Miss Loomis. "My control begins and ends in my small classroom. You would do best to leave well enough alone."

Karen slumped away from Miss Loomis's desk and back to her own.

"Why is Miss Loomis so afraid?" whispered Karen.

"The mean boys tease her, too," whispered Lisa.

For the rest of the month, the playground war just became more complicated. Lisa and Karen were now fighting for Miss Loomis, too. Yet the war was put on hold to celebrate Valentine's Day. Mrs. Duke's classroom had been transformed into a valentine wonderland. Red valentines decorated the bulletin boards. Red valentines hung from the ceiling. A red tablecloth draped the food table, which contained chocolate cupcakes frosted with red icing, a red velvet cake, red cinnamon hearts, chocolate kisses, and multicolored candy hearts. But most important were the shoeboxes that the students had decorated with red construction paper and valentines. On the top of the shoeboxes were the students' names and slits for the receipt of valentines.

Once the party started, the students went from box to box delivering their valentines to classmates. Once the boxes were full, the students took their boxes back to their desks to read the valentines that they had received.

Valentine's Day was Lisa's favorite holiday. As this year's valentine theme, Lisa chose the cartoon characters from the *Peanuts* comic strip. She delivered valentines depicting Charlie Brown, Lucy, Linus, Sally, Schroeder, Pig-Pen, Snoopy, and Woodstock to all her classmates, even Will and David. In turn, Lisa received valentines from most, if not all, of her classmates. She received two "Guess Who?" valentines. One of these anonymous valentines was addressed to "Miss Smushed Nose," so Lisa assumed that it was from Will or David. The second "Guess Who?" valentine read, "Valentine, be mine!" Did Lisa have a secret admirer, or was this just another cruel joke? Only time would tell.

Lisa took her box of valentines home to show Harold and Mark. Ozella had made heart-shaped butter cookies sprinkled with red sugar. Lisa passed out homemade valentines to Harold, Mark, baby Elizabeth, her mother and father, and Ozella. Lisa's father had purchased a special valentine for Lisa. The card read, "To My Sis." Lisa's father used his pen to change the word "Sis" to "Sissy." He gave the card to Lisa. She loved it and gave him a big hug.

Karen took her box of valentines home to show her mother. Her mother had baked heart-shaped cookies that were frosted with red icing. Karen gave her mother a special valentine. Over a month ago, Karen had sent her father a valentine in Vietnam. Today, Karen's mother gave Karen a letter from Karen's father. Karen smiled with delight. She opened the envelope and read the letter from her father. He had received her valentine and wished her "Happy Valentine's Day." Karen loved the valentine letter and gave her mother a big hug. She cried inside because she could not give her father a hug.

A half-moon shone down on Karen that Valentine's Day. That same moon shone down on Karen's father in the rice paddies of Vietnam. Karen longed for the day when she and her father would be reunited and that half-moon would become full to overflowing.

While Lisa was getting dressed for school the next day, her mother came into her bedroom. She was holding the valentine envelope that said "Miss Smushed Nose." Lisa was horrified. Now the secret about Will and David would be out, and Lisa's life would be over. Or so it seemed.

"Who gave you this card?" asked her mother.

"I-I-I don't know," stammered Lisa. "Just someone in my class making a joke."

"Well, I don't like this one bit," said Lisa's mother. "And I intend to get to the bottom of this."

"It's just a classroom prank," said Lisa.

"No," said Lisa's mother. "I know your class, and no one would dare to tease you in this way."

"Really, Mother, it's fine," said Lisa.

Lisa was starting to get a nervous stomach. She was afraid of what her mother might do.

"No," said Lisa's mother. "This has never happened before, and there's only one explanation for it—your Negro teacher sent this card to you."

"No, Mama," cried Lisa. "Miss Loomis would never do this."

"That race doesn't have any tact or manners—ignorance, pure ignorance."

"Miss Loomis is always nice to me, Mama," cried Lisa. "She would never send this card."

"Now I finally have a way to get her fired," said Lisa's mother.

"Miss Loomis couldn't have sent the card because her room is at the other end of the hall, and she didn't come in our room during the Valentine's Day party," said Lisa.

"The ways of the Negro are devious, child," said Lisa's mother.

"Mother, I beg you, please don't do anything to get Miss Loomis fired," cried Lisa.

"All right, Sissy," said Lisa's mother. "But I'm warning you. She has two strikes already—strike one was having the audacity to come to your school to teach. Strike two was sending you this card. One more strike, and she's out."

"Yes, ma'am, I understand," said Lisa. "I appreciate you giving her another chance."

"Well, finish getting dressed," said Lisa's mother. "And not a word of this to your father."

"Yes, ma'am," said Lisa.

Another secret. Lisa was about to burst. And burst she did during homeroom that morning. Cathy and Karen noticed that Lisa looked different.

"Lisa, is anything wrong?" asked Cathy.

"What happened, Lisa?" asked Karen. "You look scared."

"It's nothing, really," said Lisa. "Just a stomachache."

"Now, Lisa," said Cathy, "I know that your stomach-aches happen for a reason."

"Yeah," said Karen, "tell us what caused your stom-achache."

"But my mother made me promise not to tell," said Lisa.

"You know that you can trust us to keep your secret," said Cathy.

"Please tell us what happened," said Karen.

Lisa took a deep breath and began.

"I received a valentine addressed to 'Miss Smushed Nose,'" said Lisa. "Inside, the valentine said, 'Guess Who?' The writing on the envelope and valentine was printed so that you couldn't tell who wrote it."

"I'm sure it was Will or David," said Cathy. "What a mean thing to do."

"I agree," said Lisa. "The problem is my mother found the envelope, and she thinks that Miss Loomis wrote it. She wants to have Miss Loomis fired for sending it."

"Miss Loomis!" exclaimed Karen. "She would never do a thing like that."

"Did you tell your mom that it was Will or David?" asked Cathy.

"I didn't use any names," said Lisa. "I just said that someone in my class was playing a joke."

"All you had to do was say Will's or David's name, and your mom would've left Miss Loomis alone," said Karen.

"It's not that simple," said Lisa. "My mom always jumps to the wrong conclusion. Besides, she believes that no one in my class sent me the card."

"Well, doesn't she know that Will and David call you that name on the playground?" asked Cathy.

"No, she doesn't know anything about Will and David," said Lisa.

"Why not?" asked Cathy.

"Will said that he would hurt me if I told on him," said Lisa. "Both of you must now promise not to tell on him either."

"Why?" asked Karen.

"Because Will could hurt you and me if you tell on him," said Lisa.

"I promise," said Cathy.

"I don't like it, but I promise, too," said Karen.

"The good news," said Lisa, "is that my mother promised to leave Miss Loomis alone this time."

"My word," said Karen, "you have had a troubling morning."

"Guess what," said Lisa.

"What?" asked Cathy.

"I don't have a stomachache anymore," Lisa said. "Talking to both of you made me feel better."

Lisa really did feel better, and she breezed through her morning classes. But lunchtime proved more taxing.

Seats in the lunchroom were assigned. Mrs. Duke placed the best-behaved students with the worst-behaved students in the hopes that some of the qualities of the good students would rub off onto the bad students. Good students Lisa, Clara, and Becky were thus placed at the same table as bad students Will and David. Mrs.

Duke's strategy backfired when Will began asking probing questions of Lisa.

"I know what's wrong with you," said Will.

"Be quiet, Will," said Clara.

"Yeah, we know what's wrong with you," said David.

Lisa looked down at her plate of food and began to feel sick to her stomach.

"What are you talking about?" asked Becky.

"I know why Lisa's lip looks like it does," said Will. "My father told me."

Lisa felt her deep, dark secret slowly see the light of day. All those years of hiding in the shadows would be over in one fell swoop. No one would like her anymore. She would be the latest freak in the freak show. And it was all because of Will.

"Lisa is a harelip," said Will.

The horrible word had finally been said. The word "harelip" was as painful for Lisa to hear as the word "nigger" was for Miss Loomis to hear. Lisa began to cry. She could not make eye contact with anyone at the table.

"Stop it, Will," said Clara.

"Lisa doesn't have a hairy lip," said Becky.

"No, stupid," said Will, "Lisa's lip looks like the split lip of an H-A-R-E, a rabbit, to be exact."

"Yes, Lisa the Harelip will be able to hop on down the bunny trail this Easter," said David.

"Do the bunny hop," said Will.

"Hop, hop, hop," said David.

"You've gone too far this time, Will and David," said Clara as she stood up.

Clara walked straight to the teacher's table to get Mrs. Duke. As Mrs. Duke and Clara walked to Lisa's table, Clara told Mrs. Duke what Will and David had said to Lisa.

"Lisa a harelip?" said Mrs. Duke. "Well, I never!"

"That's not the point," said Clara. "Will and David really upset Lisa."

Clara and Mrs. Duke finally reached the lunch table, and Mrs. Duke could see that Lisa was crying.

"Lisa, honey," said Mrs. Duke, "say it isn't so—you're not really a harelip, are you?"

"Why is Mrs. Duke using that mean word?" thought Lisa, who continued to cry.

"Lisa, are you a harelip?" asked Mrs. Duke.

"Yes, ma'am," replied Lisa softly.

"Well, I never would have believed it," said Mrs. Duke while batting her eyelashes.

"What about Will and David?" asked Clara.

"I cannot punish the boys for telling the truth," said Mrs. Duke. "Now finish eating—lunch period is almost over."

Mrs. Duke walked back to the teachers' table. Lisa and Clara were dumbstruck. Telling a teacher about Will and David had backfired. Will was still the king of the table, and David held the keys to the kingdom.

After lunch Lisa went to the girls' bathroom, where she splashed water on her tear-stained face. She looked at her face in the mirror. Her eyes were red from crying. But her focus was her lip—her harelip. Cathy and Karen walked into the bathroom. Clara had told them what had happened at lunch.

"Now, now, it's all right, Lisa," said Cathy.

"Will and David are just big bullies," said Karen. "They don't know who you really are."

Lisa stopped crying. She had two good friends in Cathy and Karen.

"I've been meaning to tell you what's wrong with me," said Lisa.

"There's nothing wrong with you," said Cathy. "You are perfect just the way you are."

"Why, just look at how beautiful you look in the mirror," said Karen.

Lisa smiled at Cathy and Karen. And Lisa's world didn't come tumbling down just because Will and David called her a harelip. Cathy and Karen liked her just the way she was.

And so did Miss Loomis. Lisa could not wait for sixth period to begin. Today was the day that Miss Loomis would hand out the list of words to study for the spelling bee, which would be held in mid-April. Lisa's father said that he would call out words for her to spell every night after dinner. Lisa could hardly wait for the bee—she loved to spell.

Lisa noticed immediately that Miss Loomis didn't seem to be herself this afternoon. She did not make eye contact with any of her students, and her hands shook when she passed out the word lists.

"What could have happened to Miss Loomis?" thought Lisa.

Then Lisa got that sick feeling in the pit of her stomach. Her mother.

"Did Mother accuse Miss Loomis of sending the mean valentine?" thought Lisa. "Surely not. Mother promised not to do anything."

But something was wrong. When Becky raised her hand in class, Miss Loomis ignored her. This had never happened before. When Cathy tried to read her book report to the class, Miss Loomis postponed it. This had never happened before. When Lisa tried to read aloud during reading group, Miss Loomis told the group to read silently. This had never happened before.

"It's as if Miss Loomis is a million miles away," thought Lisa. "I wonder what's bothering her."

"Lisa," whispered Miss Loomis during reading group, "I need to see you after class."

"Yes, ma'am," said Lisa.

Lisa's palms began to sweat, her heart began to race, and she began to breathe very quickly.

"Mother must have accused Miss Loomis of sending the mean valentine," thought Lisa.

Lisa remained after class. Miss Loomis walked over to her and sat in an adjoining desk.

"Lisa, I'm here to apologize to you for sending the unkind valentine," said Miss Loomis while trembling.

"Miss Loomis," said Lisa, "you didn't send me that valentine—Will or David did. They tease me like they tease you."

"I take full responsibility for the unfortunate valentine," said Miss Loomis.

Lisa began to cry.

"I'm not like my mother, Miss Loomis," said Lisa. "I'm so sorry she accused you of this."

"It's all right, Lisa," said Miss Loomis. "To fit in at Wyatt I have to do things the way that other people want me to do them."

"In my heart I know that you did not send that valentine," said Lisa. "In my heart I know that you are the best teacher at Wyatt."

Miss Loomis smiled at Lisa. They shared what many people would believe was an unholy bond. They were both victims. They were both victims of teasing at the hands of Will and David. And they were both victims of manipulators. In Lisa's case, she was the victim of her mother's attempts to have Miss Loomis fired. Lisa was too afraid of her mother to tell her father what her mother said. In Miss Loomis's case, she was the victim of her reverend's attempts to keep her at Wyatt. Miss Loomis was too afraid of disappointing the reverend to tell anyone what the reverend said. In any case, being victims was exacting a heavy toll on Lisa and Miss Loomis. It would be a trying spring.

That evening Miss Loomis told Reverend Reed that she had been called to the principal's office.

"Today was the last straw," said Miss Loomis. "I can no longer teach at Wyatt."

"Calm down, Sister," said Reverend Reed, "and tell me what happened."

"Principal Breen told me that Lisa Parker's mother had accused me of sending Lisa a valentine that was addressed to 'Miss Smushed Nose.'"

"What does 'smushed nose' mean?" asked Reverend Reed.

"Lisa's nose is slightly flattened on one side," said Miss Loomis.

"Tell me all about it," said Reverend Reed.

"I told Principal Breen that I did not send that valentine," said Miss Loomis.

"Good," said Reverend Reed. "And then what happened?"

"Principal Breen told me that he had to take Mrs. Parker's word as the truth," said Miss Loomis, "and that if I did not apologize to Lisa for sending the valentine, I would be fired."

"I see," said Reverend Reed. "And what did you do?"

"I remembered what you told me," said Miss Loomis. "You said that I must keep my job at Wyatt at all costs. So I apologized to Lisa and kept my job."

"Good girl, Sister," said Reverend Reed. "You did the right thing today. A white lie to help the movement is always in order."

"You don't understand," said Miss Loomis. "Lisa is my favorite pupil. My apology caused me to lose face with my star student. I just can't go back and face her again."

"Face her you will," said Reverend Reed. "You have made tremendous strides at Wyatt—we can't go backward now."

"Let one of the young colored teachers take my place," said Miss Loomis.

"Say 'black,' not 'colored,'" said Reverend Reed. "No,

we can't be sending a young black teacher sporting an Afro and saying 'black power' and 'black is beautiful' to Wyatt. The movement needs you, Sister Loomis. All you did was tell a little white lie."

"All right," said Miss Loomis. "I won't quit now, but I won't be back next year."

"We'll see, Sister Loomis, we'll see," said Reverend Reed. "The Lord always provides a way."

It was mid-April, and the sixth grade was buzzing about the spelling bee. Lisa had been studying the list of words every night with her father.

"Sissy," said Mr. Parker, "spell 'architect.'"

"'Architect,' A-R-C-H-I-T-E-C-T, 'architect,'" said Lisa proudly.

"Sissy," said Mr. Parker, "My work is done. I think you are ready for the class-wide bee tomorrow."

"'Bee,'" said Harold, "B-E-E, 'bee.'"

"Very good, Bubba," said Mr. Parker.

"Does a spelling bee sting?" asked Harold.

"No, Bubba," said Lisa. "It is a contest to see who can spell the most words without making a mistake."

"Sissy's going to win," said Harold. "She knows the most words."

"Thanks, Bubba," said Lisa. "You're my biggest cheerleader."

"Time for bed," said Mr. Parker. "Sissy's got a big day tomorrow."

Lisa got ready for bed. Although she seemed too excited to sleep, she soon drifted off. Lisa dreamed that Miss Loomis turned into a huge balloon at the Macy's

Thanksgiving Day Parade. The balloon looked like Miss Loomis, and it towered over onlookers. In Lisa's dream the Miss Loomis balloon was wedged between the Snoopy balloon on one side and the Santa Claus balloon on the other side. All of a sudden in Lisa's dream the Miss Loomis balloon exploded in midair, sending fragments of balloon back to earth while clouds of helium floated upward. Lisa remembered this dream when she awoke.

"I don't want anything to happen to Miss Loomis," thought Lisa.

Lisa's mother entered her room carrying a dress. It was a white dress with a pastel paisley scarf encircling the hipline.

"What's wrong, Lisa?" her mother asked. "You look upset."

"Just a bad dream," said Lisa.

"I have a new dress for you to wear tomorrow," said Lisa's mother.

"But I don't understand," said Lisa. "The class-wide bee is today."

"I know, silly," said Lisa's mother. "You can wear your Sunday dress with the pink flowers on it today. The new dress is for the championship bee tomorrow."

Lisa could feel herself getting tense. Memories of the pageant dress flooded her brain. Money spent on a useless dress. Hopes dashed in the name of beauty.

"But, Mother," said Lisa, "this could be like the pageant dress all over again. I may not win today."

"Of course you will win today, Sissy," said Lisa's

mother. "Your winning the class-wide bee is based upon your memorization skills, not your beauty."

Lisa began to get a nervous stomach. The pressure of winning today just became enormous.

"Thanks, Mom," said Lisa tensely. "The new dress is beautiful. I hope to wear it tomorrow."

"You need to do more than hope," said Lisa's mother. "Think positive—you will wear the new dress tomorrow."

Lisa's mother left the room, and Lisa began to get dressed for the class-wide bee. Lisa wore her Sunday dress with the pink flowers on it. The dress had a fitted bustline, short sleeves, and a medium-sized print of shell-pink flowers on an ecru background. Lisa's padded bra made the dress fit perfectly, and Lisa wore a shell-pink ribbon in her hair to match her dress. To complete the ensemble Lisa also wore shell-pink Sunday shoes.

Miss Loomis designed the bee for the three classes of sixth graders. Each class would compete for a winner, and the three winners would compete the following day for the championship. Parents were not allowed to watch the class-wide competitions. The parents of the three winners would be allowed to watch the championship bee.

That morning during homeroom, Lisa talked to Cathy and Karen about the bee.

"I know you'll win, Lisa," said Cathy. "You've been studying those word lists night and day."

"Thanks," said Lisa, "but you two have as much of a chance of winning as I do."

"Guess what," said Karen. "I got a letter from my dad wishing me luck in the bee."

"That's great, Karen," said Lisa. "You can spell your way to victory."

"No, Lisa," said Karen, "you can spell *your* way to victory."

"Fair enough," said Lisa, "fair enough."

The day seemed to drag along until finally sixth period arrived and with it Lisa's class-wide bee. The students sat neatly in their desks as Miss Loomis went over the rules of the bee. Miss Loomis would call the name of a student, and the student would stand. Miss Loomis would pronounce the word to be spelled, and the student would pronounce the word, spell the word, and pronounce the word again. If correct, the student would remain standing. If incorrect, the student would sit down. Before spelling the word, the student could ask for the definition of the word and ask that the word be used in a sentence.

Miss Loomis went alphabetically down the roster calling on students to spell words. In the first round, out of twenty-four students, only eleven remained standing. Lisa made it easily through the first round by correctly spelling the word "discrimination."

"Only a colored cuddler could spell that word," said Will, who was sitting down.

"Yeah, a colored cuddler," said David, who was also seated.

Miss Loomis just heard the dreaded phrase "colored cuddler" spoken not once, but twice in her class. Her palms began to sweat, her heart began to race, and a wave of nausea rose inside her.

"Oh, Lordy, Lordy," thought Miss Loomis, "why are those boys provoking me? What would Dr. King do? Just ignore them. Yes, he would ignore them."

"This spelling bee is rigged in favor of colored cuddlers," said Will.

"Yeah, colored cuddlers," said David.

Miss Loomis just heard the dreaded phrase spoken two more times. The phrase "colored cuddler" was now echoing inside her brain, giving her a migraine headache. It was becoming impossible for Miss Loomis to ignore Will and David.

"Please make the boys stop, Lord," Miss Loomis silently prayed. "Please make them stop."

But the boys continued their racist ridicule of the spelling bee.

"Will, please use the word 'discrimination' in a sentence," joked David.

"There is a lot of discrimination against Miss Loomis at Wyatt Elementary School," joked Will.

"Will, please define the word 'discrimination,'" joked David.

"Discrimination is what white people do to Negroes to keep them in their place," said Will.

"Can't ignore anymore, can't ignore anymore," thought Miss Loomis.

Miss Loomis's head was now throbbing, and she felt like throwing up. Her headache made her thoughts repetitive.

"Stop the boys, stop the boys," she thought. "Get back to the bee, the bee."

"Boys, settle down," said Miss Loomis. "'Down,' D-O-W-N, 'down.'"

Miss Loomis looked scared. Very scared. She now had trouble holding the word list because her hands were shaking. The students were staring at her. Will and David were laughing.

"Something is wrong, really wrong," thought Miss Loomis.

"We will now begin the second round, the second . . ." said Miss Loomis in a high-pitched, nervous voice. "Karen, please spell the word 'gigantic.'"

"'Gigantic,' G-I-G-A-N-T-I-C, 'gigantic,'" said Karen.

"Co-correct," said Miss Loomis. "Cathy, please spell the word 'ballad.'"

"'Ballad,' B-A-L-L-U-D, 'ballad,'" said Cathy.

"I'm sorry, sorry, that's incorrect," said Miss Loomis. "The correct spelling is B-A-L-L-A-D."

Cathy sat down and brought with her her hopes of winning the bee.

"Clara, please spell the word 'spectacle,'" said Miss Loomis.

"'Spectacle,' S-P-E-C-T-A-C-L-E, 'spectacle,'" said Clara.

"Correct," said Miss Loomis. "Jeff, spell, spell the word 'battalion.'"

"Would you give me the definition of the word?" asked Jeff.

"Let me look it up, up in the dictionary. All right,

left, right, a battalion is a large company of soldiers ready for combat," said Miss Loomis.

"Would you use the word in a sentence?" asked Jeff.

"The battalion was camped near enemy lines," said Miss Loomis.

"'Battalion, B-A-T-T-A-L-E-O-N, 'battalion,'" said Jeff.

"That's incorrect, incorrect," said Miss Loomis. "The correct spelling is B-A-T-T-A-L-I-O-N."

"Karen's father is in a battalion captured behind enemy lines," said Will.

"Captured, POW," said David.

"He is not," said Karen. "Take that back."

"Make me," said Will.

"Children, stop this fighting at once, twice," said Miss Loomis while frantically trying to regain control of her classroom. "Lisa, spell the word 'reticent.'"

"Would you please give me the definition of the word?" asked Lisa.

"Let me look it up in the dictionary," said Miss Loomis. "Here we go, go, go. 'Reticent' means 'shy' or 'retiring.'"

"Would you please use the word in a sentence?" asked Lisa.

"The reticent girl did not want to go, go, go to school," said Miss Loomis.

"'Reticent,' R-E-T-I-C-E-N-T, 'reticent,'" said Lisa.

"Correct," said Miss Loomis.

"Lisa's reticent, all right," said Will. "She's reticent because of her harelip."

"Do the bunny hop," said David. "Hop, hop, hop."

"That's the last straw, turkey in the straw," thought Miss Loomis.

"Will, apologize to Lisa right, right now," said Miss Loomis.

"I don't apologize for the truth," said Will.

"It's all right, Miss Loomis," said Lisa. "It is true that I was born with a cleft palate and cleft lip."

"I know, know, honey," said Miss Loomis, "but the word 'harelip' is mean, mean, and Will owes you an apology."

"No apology from me," said Will. "David, would you use the words 'reticent' and 'harelip' in a sentence, please?"

"The colored cuddler was reticent on account of her harelip," said David.

"Very good," said Will.

"I am the teacher, and you are the students," said Miss Loomis in a trembling voice.

"No Negro will ever be my teacher," said Will.

"I am the teacher!" screamed Miss Loomis.

The class became silent. Will and David were quiet for the moment. The only sound Ms. Loomis could hear was the silent screaming in her own brain.

With each round of the spelling bee, Miss Loomis became more and more unglued. She began to perspire heavily, and rings of sweat were visible under the arms of her pastel yellow dress. Her nervous twitches took their toll on her bun, which became more and more disheveled. With each comment that Will or David made, Miss Loomis extracted another bobby pin from her bun. She lined up her bobby pins in a row as if they were an army lining up for battle. But war she did not wage.

Out of a field of eleven students in the second round, only three remained for the final round of the class-wide bee—Karen, Clara, and Lisa. Miss Loomis had become so anxious that she had to sit down at her desk for the final round. She held her word list in her trembling hands as a spitball hit her in the face. Then another. Miss Loomis took a deep breath.

"What would Dr. King do if he were here today?" thought Miss Loomis. "He would practice nonviolence, and so must I."

Yet Miss Loomis took Dr. King's practice of nonviolence to the extreme. She became helpless in the face of Will and David's comments. Miss Loomis began the final round of the class-wide bee in a complete state of disarray. Her voice was high-pitched, her hands were trembling, and her hair had fallen out of its bun.

"Karen, please spell the word 'transient,'" said Miss Loomis.

"Would you please give me the definition of the word?" asked Karen.

"Let me look it up, up, up in the dictionary. 'Transient' means 'temporary, lasting only a moment,'" said Miss Loomis.

"Would you please use the word in a sentence?" asked Karen.

"Her fears were as transient as the sunset," said Miss Loomis.

"'Transient,' T-R-A-N-S-I-A-N-T, 'transient,'" said Karen.

"I'm sorry, sorry, that's incorrect," said Miss Loomis.

"The correct spelling is T-R-A-N-S-I-E-N-T, 'transient.'"

Karen sat down, leaving only Clara and Lisa.

"Lisa," said Miss Loomis, "spell the word 'licentious.'"

"Would you please define the word?" asked Lisa.

"Let me look it up in the dictionary, the dictionary. 'Licentious' means 'lacking in legal or moral restraints,'" said Miss Loomis.

"Would you use the word in a sentence?" asked Lisa.

"The licentious behavior of the prisoners caused turmoil," said Miss Loomis.

"'Licentious,' L-I-C-E-N-T-I-O-U-S, 'licentious,'" said Lisa.

"That's correct," said Miss Loomis.

Lisa remained standing.

"Clara, please spell the word 'deprecate,'" said Miss Loomis.

"Would you please define the word?" asked Clara.

"Let me look it up, down, up in the dictionary. 'Deprecate' means 'to disapprove of, often in a mild way,'" said Miss Loomis.

"Would you use the word in a sentence?" asked Clara.

"The quiet man deprecated loud parades," said Miss Loomis.

"'Deprecate,' D-E-P-R-A-C-A-T-E, 'deprecate.'"

"I'm sorry, that's incorrect," said Miss Loomis. "The correct spelling is D-E-P-R-E-C-A-T-E."

Clara sat down, and Lisa was the only student left standing. A spitball hit Lisa in the face. Another spitball hit Miss Loomis. Will and David were laughing.

"Lisa," said Miss Loomis, "it is my pleasure to inform

you that you are the winner, winner, winner of the class-wide bee. Congratulations. You will compete tomorrow in the championship bee. Class, give Lisa a round, round, round of applause."

As the class applauded, Will and David became more out of control.

"David, spell the word 'Negro,'" said Will.

"Would you give me the definition?" asked David.

"A Negro is a person with black skin and kinky hair who talks funny and smells bad and lives in the quarter," said Will.

"Would you use the word in a sentence?" asked David.

"The Negro teacher quit teaching at the white school," said Will.

"'Negro,' N-I-G-G-E-R, 'Negro,'" said David.

"You are correct," said Will.

Miss Loomis stared at her list of words and said the word "Negro." She then began to talk uncontrollably. The words of Dr. King raced through her brain like a runaway locomotive. She began to speak as if in a trance.

"I want to have a dream, but white folks givin' me nightmares.

"Sweet Jesus, I want to overcome Negro, Negress.

"I want blacker skin, not mulatto or high yellow.

"I had a dream.

"Wind blew it away."

Lisa walked over to Miss Loomis, who was now crying. Lisa could feel Miss Loomis slowly slipping away like that Macy's Thanksgiving Day balloon. Her cries soon became sobs.

"I can't t-t-take this anymore," sobbed Miss Loomis. "I j-j-just can't take this."

"What can I do to help?" asked Lisa.

"Call Re-Re-Reverend Reed," sobbed Miss Loomis. "Principal Breen has his nu-nu-number."

Sadly, Lisa felt herself grow stronger as Miss Loomis grew weaker. Lisa wanted to protect Miss Loomis at all costs. Even the cost of facing Will and David.

"Karen, Clara," said Lisa, "go to the principal's office for help."

Karen and Clara immediately left Miss Loomis's room for the principal's office. Cathy walked up to Miss Loomis's desk.

"What can I do to help?" asked Cathy.

"Just sit here beside Miss Loomis and pat her hand," said Lisa. "I've got some business to attend to."

Lisa walked up to Will and David, who were sitting at their desks. Lisa was scared, and her hands were shaking.

"Will and David," said Lisa, "you owe Miss Loomis an apology, so get up and go apologize right now."

"No," said Will. "We don't take orders from harelips."

Tears stung Lisa's eyes. Will had used the dreaded word once again.

"Now you owe me an apology, too," said Lisa.

"Never," said Will.

"Never," said David.

"We don't apologize for the truth," said Will. "Miss Loomis is a Negro, and you are a harelip."

"Yeah," said David.

"Miss Loomis is upset," said Lisa. "The word 'harelip'

and the word N-I-G-G-E-R are meant to hurt feelings, not tell the truth. So you do owe us an apology."

At that moment the class bell rang, and all of the students except Lisa and Cathy filed out of Miss Loomis's room. Lisa and Cathy continued to comfort Miss Loomis, who continued to cry.

"Please don't let Will and David make you sad," said Lisa. "They're just big bullies who pick on everyone."

"That's right," said Cathy. "Why, they hurt Lisa's feelings all the time."

"But I'm not going to let them win the bully game," said Lisa.

"I'm not on home base—I'm out," said Miss Loomis. "I'm out—Will and David won."

"Miss Loomis," said Cathy, "you're not making any sense."

"Cents—I have dollars and cents," said Miss Loomis.

"Just focus on your word list," said Lisa. "Everything is going to be all right."

"Left, right, left, right, march," said Miss Loomis. "March, April, May."

"May I come in?" asked Principal Breen, who had been standing at the door.

"In and out and out and in—I'm in a tailspin," said Miss Loomis.

"Girls, you need to go on home—I will take care of Miss Loomis," said Principal Breen.

"Who is Miss Loomis?" asked Miss Loomis. "I don't see her anywhere."

Lisa and Cathy were very confused. Lisa began to cry, and Cathy continued to pat Miss Loomis's hand.

"Girls," said Principal Breen.

Lisa and Cathy each gave Miss Loomis a hug before leaving the room. Once outside, they began to discuss the situation.

"What's wrong with Miss Loomis?" asked Cathy.

"She's very upset," said Lisa. "I'm scared for her—she was talking nonsense."

"I know," said Cathy. "I just hope she will be all right."

"I just hope that Will and David are ashamed of what they did," said Lisa. "Miss Loomis may very well quit now."

"I hope she doesn't quit," said Cathy.

"So do I, Cathy. So do I," said Lisa.

Mrs. Parker and Harold were waiting for Lisa after school. Lisa got into the front seat of the car without saying a word.

"Well," said Mrs. Parker, "did you win the class-wide bee?"

"Yes, ma'am, I did," said Lisa.

"Sissy won! Sissy won!" exclaimed Harold.

"That's wonderful, Sissy," said Mrs. Parker. "I just knew you would. Now you get to wear your new dress tomorrow."

"That's right," said Lisa.

"Well, you don't seem very happy about it," said Mrs. Parker. "Is something wrong?"

"Yes," said Lisa. "Will and David started teasing Miss Loomis, and she started crying. The bell rang, but Cathy and I stayed with Miss Loomis until the principal got there. I don't know what will happen to her."

"Well, I never heard of such sensitivity," said Mrs. Parker. "What did Will and David say?"

"They called her a Negro but pretended like it was one of the spelling-bee words and spelled the word N-I-G-G-E-R instead," said Lisa.

"Oh, that's nothing," said Mrs. Parker. "There's something wrong with a teacher who doesn't have the respect of her students."

"There's nothing wrong with Miss Loomis," said Lisa. "She is a wonderful teacher. Will and David are bullies and should be punished."

"I've known Will and David since they were babies, and they are not bullies," said Mrs. Parker.

"Oh, yes they are," said Lisa. "I've seen them bully other children in my class."

"Who?" asked Mrs. Parker.

"Will and David teased Clara Martin about her weak eyes, and Will broke her glasses with a dodgeball," said Lisa.

"Well you girls shouldn't have been playing dodgeball with the boys," said Mrs. Parker. "Anyway, Miss Loomis had no business teaching at Wyatt, so it would be for the best that she quit."

"Mother, how can you say such a horrible thing?" said Lisa.

"Besides, her crying today counts as strike three, and

she's out of Wyatt if I have anything to do with it," said Mrs. Parker.

"Please don't do anything, Mother," said Lisa.

"Don't worry," said Mrs. Parker. "I'll let nature take its course. And not a word of this to your father."

"Yes, ma'am," said Lisa.

That evening at dinner, Mr. Parker noticed that something was wrong with Lisa. While Mrs. Parker escorted Harold and Mark to take their baths, he sat down next to Lisa.

"For someone who just won the class-wide bee, you seem to be awfully sad," said Mr. Parker. "What's wrong, Sissy?"

Lisa's eyes filled with tears, and she began to cry.

"Oh, it's just awful, Daddy," said Lisa. "Will and David teased Miss Loomis, and she began to cry. The principal had to come and everything."

"Now, now," said Mr. Parker. "I'll just call Principal Breen and see what happened."

Mrs. Parker walked back into the dining room.

"Well, I don't see why you need to involve yourself in the affairs of a Negro school teacher," said Mrs. Parker.

"Don't get started, Penelope," said Mr. Parker. "Miss Loomis may need our help."

Lisa finished eating while her father called Principal Breen. She had another nervous stomach and had difficulty swallowing her food. Her father soon returned to tell her the news.

"It's more serious than I thought," said Mr. Parker.

"Miss Loomis's doctor wants her to rest for the next two months, so a substitute teacher is taking over her classes. The championship bee will still be held tomorrow."

"Say it's not so, Daddy, say it's not so," cried Lisa. "I don't know what I'll do without Miss Loomis."

"You'll do just fine, Sissy, you'll do just fine," said Mr. Parker. "Why, look what you have done this past year. You don't check out of school with stomachaches anymore. You've grown into a brave young lady who can win the championship bee tomorrow."

"Do you really think so, Daddy?" Lisa asked.

"Of course I do," said Mr. Parker. "Why don't you win the bee tomorrow for Miss Loomis. She would be so proud of you."

"I will, Daddy, I will," said Lisa. "I'll do it for Miss Loomis."

That night before going to sleep, Lisa said a prayer for Miss Loomis. She prayed extra hard so that her prayer might be answered. Lisa went to sleep and dreamed that Miss Loomis was the only Negro soldier in a battalion of white soldiers behind enemy lines. Instead of a rifle, Miss Loomis was armed with a blackboard eraser, which she used to erase the white lines of attack on the battalion's blackboard.

The next morning Lisa awoke refreshed. She seemed ready to take on the world until she thought of Miss Loomis. She became sad, but she remembered her promise to win the championship bee for Miss Loomis. She put on the new white dress and tied the pastel paisley scarf around her hips. She wore panty hose for the first time with her white Sunday shoes. She was growing up, but she was still superstitious. She rubbed her green Rat-fink eraser for luck. She also stroked the pink-and-white hair of her troll doll three times for luck.

In homeroom everyone was talking about Miss Loomis. Rumors encircled the room. Jeff Stewart said that he had heard that Miss Loomis was crazy and was staying in a mental hospital. Roxanne Phillips said that she had heard that Miss Loomis was arrested and was staying in jail. Clara Martin said that she had heard that Miss Loomis would be back next week and that the championship bee would be next week. Mrs. Duke tried to make order out of the chaos.

"Class," said Mrs. Duke, "may I have your attention?"

The students stopped their speculations long enough to hear what Mrs. Duke had to say.

"Miss Loomis is taking a leave of absence from Wyatt, effective immediately," said Mrs. Duke. "Mrs. Weaver will be your new English teacher starting today, and Mrs. Weaver will preside over the championship bee, which will be held this morning at nine o'clock in the auditorium."

"Not Mrs. Weaver," thought Lisa. "She refused to teach in a colored school. She might dislike me because my father has colored clients."

Lisa began to get a nervous stomach. Then she remembered Miss Loomis.

"I'm going to win the championship bee for Miss Loomis," thought Lisa. "Mrs. Weaver will not stand in my way."

At the end of homeroom all the sixth graders walked to the auditorium for the championship bee. As the students took their seats, Lisa walked up the steps to the stage. Joining her onstage were the other contestants, Abigail Henry from Mrs. Darren's homeroom and Charles Culver from Miss Newell's homeroom. Mrs. Weaver and Principal Breen escorted the three contestants to three folding chairs located on the right side of the stage. Mrs. Weaver and Principal Breen then sat at a table that faced the three contestants. A podium stood at the right-hand corner of the stage.

In the center of the table stood a trophy. It was a gold loving cup mounted on a wooden base. Engraved on the trophy were the words "1969 Sixth-Grade Spelling Bee Champion, Wyatt Elementary School, Montgomery, Alabama." Underneath the engraving was space to engrave the champion's name. Beside the trophy were red and yellow ribbons for second and third place. The three contestants could not take their eyes off the trophy.

Principal Breen walked to the podium and began to speak.

"May I have your attention, please," said Principal Breen. "It is my pleasure to welcome you to the sixth-grade championship spelling bee. Our three contestants are Charles Culver, Abigail Henry, and Lisa Parker. Let's give our contestants a round of applause."

While the audience was applauding, Lisa looked out to see her mother and father along with Harold and Mark seated in the third row. Mr. Parker had Lisa's list of words firmly in his hand just in case the moderator strayed from its contents. Lisa smiled at her family.

Principal Breen continued.

"As you can see, we have a trophy this year. This beautiful trophy was donated by Miss Loomis and will go to the winner of the championship bee. Presiding over this bee will be Mrs. Lottice Weaver," said Principal Breen. "Let the bee begin."

Principal Breen walked back to his seat at the table, and Mrs. Weaver walked to the podium.

"The rules of the bee are as follows," said Mrs. Weaver. "All words used in the bee must come from the list of words that Miss Loomis gave the sixth-grade students. Contestants must walk to the podium, say the word to be spelled, spell the word, and say the word again. Contestants may ask for the definition of the word to be spelled before spelling the word. Contestants may also ask that the word to be spelled be used in a sentence before spelling the word. If a contestant incorrectly spells a word, he or she will be eliminated from the bee. The last contestant remaining in the bee wins."

Mrs. Weaver walked back to her seat at the table. Directly in front of her was the list of words that Miss Loomis had given each sixth grader to study for the bees. Mrs. Weaver reached in her purse and pulled out another list of words, which she placed on top of Miss Loomis's list.

"Charles," said Mrs. Weaver, "please spell the word 'lily.'"

Charles stood up and walked to the podium. He was

wearing a navy blazer with a blue oxford cloth button-down shirt, rep tie, and khaki pants. He wore navy-and-ivory saddle shoes.

"'Lily,' L-I-L-Y, 'lily,'" said Charles.

"Correct," said Mrs. Weaver. "Abby, please spell the word 'daisy.'"

Charles left the podium as Abby approached it. Abby was wearing a navy short-sleeved dress piped in red. She wore red shoes and had a red ribbon in her hair.

"'Daisy,' D-A-I-S-Y, 'daisy,'" said Abby.

"Correct," said Mrs. Weaver. "Lisa, please spell the word 'nasturtium.'"

Abby left the podium as Lisa stood up and walked to it. She took a deep breath.

"'Nasturtium,' N-A-S-T-U-R-T-I-U-M, 'nasturtium,'" said Lisa.

Mr. Parker stood up and faced Principal Breen.

"I want to voice my objection to this last word," said Mr. Parker. "The word 'nasturtium' is not on the list of words given to the students. Mrs. Weaver should be instructed to confine her words to those found on the appropriate word list."

"Well it doesn't matter because Lisa spelled the word correctly," said Mrs. Weaver. "I will now continue the bee. Charles, please spell the word 'ebony.'"

Mr. Parker sat down while Lisa and Charles exchanged places.

"'Ebony,' E-B-O-N-Y, 'ebony,'" said Charles.

"Correct," said Mrs. Weaver. "Abby, please spell the word 'ivory.'"

Abby walked to the podium and looked at the audience.

"'Ivory,' I-V-O-R-Y, 'ivory,'" said Abby.

"Correct," said Mrs. Weaver. "Lisa, please spell the word 'mulatto.'"

Mr. Parker rose from his seat, holding the word list in midair.

"Objection," said Mr. Parker. "This word is not only not on the word list, but it is also the rankest form of racism I know. Mrs. Weaver should be removed from this panel at once."

"Your objection is well founded," said Principal Breen. "Mrs. Weaver, please give Lisa an appropriate word."

"Lisa, please spell the word 'anxiety.'"

Mr. Parker sat back down, and Lisa went to the podium.

"'Anxiety,' A-N-X-I-E-T-Y, 'anxiety,'" said Lisa.

"Correct," said Mrs. Weaver. "Charles, please spell the word 'dolor.'"

Lisa left the podium as Charles walked to it.

"May I have the definition of the word, please?" asked Charles.

"'Dolor' means 'sorrow,'" said Mrs. Weaver.

"Would you please use the word in a sentence?" asked Charles.

"Dolor and tears accompanied the funeral," said Mrs. Weaver.

"Dolor, D-O-L-E-R, dolor," said Charles.

"I'm sorry," said Mrs. Weaver, "that's incorrect. The

correct spelling is D-O-L-O-R. Round two between Abby and Lisa will now commence."

The Parker family smiled up at Lisa. Lisa was poised for victory.

"Lisa, please spell the word 'perspicacious,'" said Mrs. Weaver.

Lisa walked to the podium. She knew the word—it was one of the words she had studied with her father. She didn't need the definition of the word. She didn't need to have the word used in a sentence. She was ready to spell the word.

"'Perspicacious,' P-E-R-S-P-I-C-A-C-I-O-U-S, 'perspicacious,'" said Lisa.

"Correct," said Mrs. Weaver. "Abby, please spell the word 'torpor.'"

Abby walked to the podium solemnly. She was unsure of the word.

"May I please have the definition of the word?" asked Abby.

"'Torpor' means 'dormancy' or 'apathy,'" said Mrs. Weaver.

"Would you use the word in a sentence?" asked Abby.

"His torpor kept him from voting," said Mrs. Weaver.

"'Torpor,' T-O-R-P-E-R, 'torpor,'" said Abby.

"I'm sorry," said Mrs. Weaver, "that's incorrect. Lisa, you are the winner of the championship bee."

Lisa stood up to the sound of applause. She was so happy. And she had done it all for Miss Loomis. The three contestants walked over to the trophy table. Principal Breen gave Abby and Charles ribbons for second and third place, respectively. With the trophy in his hands, Principal Breen walked over to the podium with Lisa.

"May I have your attention, please," said Principal Breen. "It is my pleasure to award this trophy to the nineteen sixty-nine champion of the sixth-grade spelling bee, Miss Lisa Parker."

Principal Breen handed the trophy to Lisa, who held it up for all to see. A thunderous round of applause followed. Lisa carried her trophy and walked offstage and into the audience. She was surrounded by students who were congratulating her. Then she saw her parents and brothers.

"Sissy, you won!" exclaimed Harold.

"Sissy won!" exclaimed Mark.

"Thank you so much, Bubba and Brother," said Lisa.

"I want to touch the trophy," said Harold.

"Let me," said Mark.

"Here you go, boys," said Lisa, who lowered the trophy so they could touch it.

Mr. Parker reached out to give his daughter a big hug.

"Sissy, we are so very proud of you," said Mr. Parker.

"Thank you, Daddy," Lisa said as she beamed. "I couldn't have done it without all of your help."

"And how nice of Miss Loomis to have donated the trophy," said Mr. Parker.

"I want Miss Loomis to know that I won," said Lisa.

"I'll make sure she gets the message," said Mr. Parker.

"Congratulations, Sissy," said Mrs. Parker. "Let me see your trophy. Oh, look, there's a place to have your name engraved on the trophy. I'll take it to the trophy shop to be engraved."

"Thanks, Mom," said Lisa while handing her the trophy. "I'm so glad it's over."

The Parkers escorted Harold back to class and then went home. Lisa headed for recess with Cathy and Karen. The children were playing Red Rover. The playground was divided into two opposing lines of players. The players in each line clasped hands to prevent an opposing player from breaking through their line and taking their strongest player back to the opposing line. Will and David were standing next to each other in one line, and Lisa, Cathy, and Karen were standing next to each other in the opposing line. Will was the captain of his line, and Jeff was the captain of the opposing line.

Will made the first call.

"Red Rover, Red Rover, send Cathy right over," yelled Will.

Cathy ran as fast as she could and tried to break through the line between Clara and Roxanne, the weakest link. Clara's and Roxanne's hands remained clasped, with Cathy left dangling from their arms in midair, and Cathy was forced to join Will's line.

Jeff from the opposing line made the second call.

"Red Rover, Red Rover, send Clara right over," yelled Jeff.

Clara ran as fast as she could and tried to break through the line between Lisa and Karen, the weakest link. Lisa's and Karen's hands remained clasped, with Clara left dangling from their arms in midair, and Clara was forced to join Jeff's line.

The game was tied, with the same number of players in each line. Will made the next call.

"Red Rover, Red Rover, send the harelip right over," yelled Will.

Lisa let go of Karen's hand. Tears burned her eyes, but she refused to cry. Jeff issued a reply.

"If you don't use the player's name, then you lose your turn," yelled Jeff.

"All right," barked Will. "Red Rover, Red Rover, send Lisa the Harelip right over."

Lisa felt naked before her class. There was now no doubt about it; everyone in her class knew her secret. Lisa was a harelip. But this truth set Lisa free. Lisa did not get a stomachache. She did not need to check out of school to hide from her classmates. She was free. Free to be the girl she really was, a girl with a cleft palate and cleft lip. Her classmates liked her before they knew her secret. Now they should like her even more because of the courage it took her to overcome her secret. Lisa was tough. As tough as nails.

Lisa ran as fast as she could and tried to break through the line between Roxanne and Becky, their weakest link. Roxanne's and Becky's hands remained clasped, with Lisa swinging from their arms in midair, and Lisa was forced to join Will's side. Will, the strongest link, made Lisa, the weakest link, stand next to him and hold his hand. Jeff made the next call.

"Red Rover, Red Rover, send Becky right over," yelled Jeff.

Becky ran as fast as she could and tried to break through the line between Karen and Clara, their weakest link. Karen's and Clara's hands remained clasped, with Becky dangling from their arms in midair, and Becky was forced to join Jeff's side. The game was still tied. Will made the next call.

"Red Rover, Red Rover, send Clara right over," yelled Will.

"Clara, try to break through the line between Will and me," yelled Lisa.

Clara ran as fast as she could. At the moment she was about to reach Lisa and Will, Lisa let go of Will's hand. Clara broke through the line and took Will back to Jeff's line. Jeff's line now had more players than Will's line. Will had been dethroned. He was no longer a captain but rather a captive. Turnabout was fair play.

Lisa won a lot more than the spelling bee that day. She won her freedom. She had overcome.

Chapter Twenty

The Award

During the first week of May, Miss Newell had a special announcement for Lisa's class. Miss Newell was wearing a black sleeveless dress with a pink silk scarf and black pumps. She was using her sweet voice.

"Now, class," said Miss Newell, "my sweet, sweet students, you remember that essay you wrote back in September? The one about why the death of Mr. King was for the best?"

"For the best?" asked Karen.

"Sweetie, you weren't here in September," said the sweet Miss Newell, "so you can't participate in this contest. I encouraged the children to write their essays on why Mr. King's death was for the best because of the hornet's nest he stirred up in the Negro quarter during his lifetime."

Miss Newell now changed into her mean voice.

"Well, a sixth grader from our school won the contest," barked Miss Newell. "The school board will announce the winner in the auditorium on the last day of school, and the winner will receive an award."

"Can you tell us who won?" asked Cathy.

"No, honey, I can't," said the sweet Miss Newell. "But it certainly wasn't my first choice," snarled the mean Miss Newell, who was glaring at Lisa.

Lisa smiled. For the first time she was not afraid of Miss Newell's mean voice. She remembered the essay she had written. It said that the assassination of Dr. King was for the worst. Could her essay be the winning essay? Only time would tell.

Lisa also remembered that Miss Newell called her a "colored cuddler" for honoring Dr. King in her essay. Perhaps the members of the school board did not share Miss Newell's view of her essay. Lisa could not wait to get home to tell her father about the contest and her essay. This time there would be no secrets to hide from her father.

That evening at dinner Lisa was bursting with news.

"Daddy, guess what," said Lisa.

"You won the spelling bee!" exclaimed her father.

"No, Daddy," Lisa said, "something else."

"I don't know, Sissy," said her father. "What is it?"

"Back in September the sixth grade wrote essays about the assassination of Dr. King as part of a contest sponsored by the school board," said Lisa.

"That's wonderful, Sissy," said her father.

"Well, someone from our school won the contest," said Lisa, "and the school board is going to give the winner an award in the auditorium on the last day of school."

"Well, this calls for a new dress," said her mother.

"But I may not win," said Lisa.

"Of course you'll win," said her mother. "Why, you write better than anyone in your grade."

"Thank you, Mother," said Lisa.

That night Lisa dreamed that Miss Loomis was at the Lincoln Memorial giving Dr. King's "I Have a Dream" speech before thousands. Her tiny hands turned into two white doves, which flew over the reflecting pool. She bowed before the audience at the close of her speech. Beside her was a large loom, but she could not weave any cloth because she had no hands.

Lisa remembered this dream when she awoke, and she thought of Miss Loomis. She wondered if Miss Loomis was still troubled by the mean words of Will and David. She wondered if Reverend Reed checked on Miss Loomis from time to time. She wondered if Miss Loomis would return to Wyatt in the fall. But mostly, she wondered if Miss Loomis was happy.

"In my dream," thought Lisa, "Miss Loomis is doing great things. Miss Loomis did great things at Wyatt, and I hope that she will continue to do great things. Only time will tell."

Time passed slowly during the month of May. It had been a month since Miss Loomis left, but it seemed like an eternity to Lisa. Class with Mrs. Weaver moved at a snail's pace. All of the wonder and mystery of Miss Loomis's class was gone, and in its place grew the seeds of complaisance. As long as the class cooperated with Mrs. Weaver, class would be easy. This cooperation took the form of blind obedience to Mrs. Weaver's book list. Gone was Miss Loomis's selection of *Little Women*, and in its place was Mrs. Weaver's selection of *Uncle Remus Stories.* Plantation life was once again glorified by a Wyatt teacher.

Mrs. Weaver had bleached blonde hair and wore brightly colored floral dresses. She dressed like she lived in Hawaii, not Alabama. And she said a mental "aloha" to Miss Loomis as she took the reins of sixth-grade English.

"Class," said Mrs. Weaver, "today you are going to write a one-page essay on why plantation life was for the best."

"You've got to be kidding," said Karen. "Blacks were slaves on the plantations."

"And they were often beaten to the point of death and mistreated," said Lisa.

"I was warned about you two and your liberal views," said Mrs. Weaver. "In my class, plantation life was a happy life for slave and master alike."

Lisa could not believe what Mrs. Weaver was saying. Then she remembered how she phrased the essay for Miss Newell's class.

"May we write why plantation life was for the worst?" asked Lisa.

"I don't care what you and Karen write about," said Mrs. Weaver, "but the good grades go to those who write a positive essay."

Mrs. Weaver had adopted the Pollyanna philosophy, which said that every person, place, or thing could be described in positive terms.

"That's not fair," said Lisa.

"Life is not always fair," said Mrs. Weaver.

"Well, we'll just write our essays on why freedom for the slaves was for the best," said Karen with a clever turn of phrase.

"Write it how you choose, as long as it's positive," said Mrs. Weaver.

"Thank you, ma'am," said Lisa.

Lisa and Karen wrote the only essays on why freedom for the slaves was for the best. The rest of the class wrote essays on why plantation life was for the best. Because all of the essays in Lisa's class were written from positive points of view, Mrs. Weaver awarded As to all of her students.

While Mrs. Weaver was stuck in plantation times, Mrs. Duke was preparing the students for the Apollo 11 moon landing in July. It was the last week of school. The awards ceremony was tomorrow.

"Class," said Mrs. Duke while pointing to a poster of the moon, "the astronauts studied a mean moon to aid in plotting their landing site on the real moon."

"You mean the moon is mean to the astronauts?" asked Becky. "Kind of like the way some children are mean to others on the playground?"

"No, Becky," said Mrs. Duke while batting her eyelashes.

Mrs. Duke took a model of the moon and began revolving it in her hands around a model of the earth.

"A mean moon is a make-believe moon," said Mrs. Duke. "This play moon is imagined, for purposes of calculation, to revolve around the earth uniformly as the real moon would."

"I'm confused," said Jeff. "Are the astronauts landing on a make-believe moon?"

"No, Jeff," said Mrs. Duke, "the astronauts are landing on the real moon. The mean moon just helped them chart their course."

"So the mean moon is a good thing," said Lisa.

"Yes, Lisa," said Mrs. Duke, "the mean moon is a good thing. The word 'mean' in 'mean moon' does not mean unkind or hurtful—it relates to mathematical calculations."

"That's cool," said Lisa. "And guess what—I'm eleven, and the spacecraft is named Apollo 11."

"Very good, Lisa," said Mrs. Duke, "very good. The three astronauts going into space are white men. They make the perfect team for this mission"

"Are you saying that blacks or women couldn't be astronauts on this mission?" asked Lisa.

"That's exactly what I'm saying—blacks aren't smart enough, and women are too weak to go into space," said Mrs. Duke. "Why, women and blacks can't fly planes."

"Oh, yes, they can," said Lisa. "Amelia Earhart and the Tuskegee Airmen flew planes."

"Yes, and look what happened to Miss Earhart," said Mrs. Duke. "The moon mission is clearly a job for white men."

"Well I think that one day women and blacks will go into space," said Lisa.

"Wishful thinking," said Mrs. Duke, "wishful thinking."

The discussion of the mean moon and the white astronauts carried over to the playground. Will began taunting Lisa and used the moon as his new weapon.

"I know what a mean moon really is," said Will. "It's when the astronauts jump up and down on the moon and say mean things."

"No, it's not," said Karen.

"Shut up, Miss POW," said David.

"A mean moon is when the astronauts say, 'Lisa is a harelip,' over and over," said Will.

Lisa flinched at the mention of the word "harelip," but she did not get a stomachache. She took some deep breaths and responded to the bully.

"You are confusing cruel words with a mean moon," said Lisa. "A mean moon cannot hurt me, unlike you."

"Well, you can never go to the moon because you're a girl," said Will.

"Yeah, weakling," said David.

"I predict that during my lifetime a woman will go into space," said Lisa.

"You're dreaming," said Will.

"Yeah, dreaming of castles in the sky," said David.

"No, I'm dreaming of women in the sky," said Lisa.

"You're dreaming of a harelip woman in the sky," said Will.

"Yeah, harelip," said David.

"Will and David," said Jeff, "leave Lisa alone."

"Thanks, Jeff," said Lisa.

"Well, well, well," said Will, "it seems we have two lovebirds on the playground."

"Yeah, lovebirds," said David.

Jeff turned red and replied, "I'm just sticking up for Lisa."

Lisa was dumbstruck—was Jeff the one who sent her the mushy valentine? Only time would tell.

Jeff escorted Lisa and Karen away from Will and David. There would be no more discussions of mean moons or mushy valentines that day.

That night at dinner the conversation revolved around the awards ceremony tomorrow.

"I just know you're going to win," said Lisa's mother. "I have a surprise for you."

Lisa's mother walked into the laundry room and came back with a new dress for Lisa. The sleeveless dress was navy blue with a large white collar.

"It's beautiful," said Lisa. "But I might not win."

"You have as good a chance as anyone in your grade," said Lisa's father. "Wear the dress with pride."

"Yes, sir," said Lisa.

Lisa's father smiled and winked at Lisa's mother.

That night Lisa dreamed that the moon really was mean because the man in the moon called her a harelip. Lisa awoke refreshed and wondered why there wasn't a woman in the moon, too. She put on her new dress and went to school.

It was the last day of school, and everyone was excited. At nine o'clock all of the sixth graders headed to the auditorium. Onstage were several men and women along with Miss Newell and Principal Breen. At a table on the stage was a gold medal attached to a ribbon with red, white, and blue stripes. Next to the gold medal was a piece of white notebook paper with dark cursive writing on it.

In the front row of the auditorium Lisa saw all of her family seated together. There were her parents, Harold, Mark, and Ozella, who held baby Elizabeth. Ozella was not wearing her maid's uniform; she was dressed in a black dress that was piped in white. Lisa's parents motioned for Lisa to sit beside them. Lisa sat at the end of the row next to her father.

Lisa felt a tap on her shoulder and looked up to see Miss Loomis and Reverend Reed. Lisa stood up and hugged Miss Loomis, who was wearing a navy dress with a red bow. Lisa and her family moved over two seats, and Miss Loomis and Reverend Reed sat down next to Lisa. Principal Breen was standing at the podium.

"May I have your attention, please," said Principal Breen. "I welcome you to this special awards ceremony. Last September the City of Montgomery School Board announced a contest open to all Montgomery-public-school sixth graders. Each sixth grader wrote a one-page essay on the death of Dr. Martin Luther King. The best essay as judged by the school board would be given an award the following May. Here to present the award for best essay is Dr. Rufus Carter of the City of Montgomery School Board."

An elderly Negro man with white hair and glasses took the gold medal from the table and approached the podium. He was wearing a black suit with a red tie.

"It is my pleasure to announce the winner of the essay contest—Lisa Parker, will you please come forward."

The auditorium erupted in applause as Lisa walked to the podium.

"Congratulations, Lisa," said Dr. Carter. "On behalf of the City of Montgomery School Board, I hereby bestow upon you this gold medal in recognition of your excellent essay."

Dr. Carter placed the gold medal around Lisa's neck. The audience applauded.

"Principal Breen," said Dr. Carter, "may I have Lisa's essay, please?"

Principal Breen took the piece of notebook paper from the table and handed it to Dr. Carter.

"Lisa, your essay was meant to be shared," said Dr. Carter. "Would you please read your essay to the audience?"

Dr. Carter handed the essay to Lisa. Lisa moved to the podium and stood in front of its microphone. She began to get a nervous stomach and touched her gold medal for luck.

"Yes, sir," said Lisa.

Lisa glanced down at her essay and saw trouble on the horizon. She took a deep breath and began reading aloud.

"I believe that the assassination of Dr. Martin Luther King was one of the worst experiences in our nation's history. I was born with a gaping black hole in the center of my face."

Lisa felt her face grow red with embarrassment. She had just told the world her secret. Yet, surprisingly, the earth did not fall off its axis and spin out of control. The earth continued to revolve around the sun while the moon continued to revolve around the earth. Lisa took another deep breath and continued reading.

"The assassination of Dr. King left a gaping black hole in the center of this country. Although surgery repaired my gaping black hole, there is no surgical procedure to repair the gaping black hole in this country. Dr. King sought to unite the races in friendship. His assassination seeks to divide the races as enemies. Only the principle of racial equality can begin to close the gaping black hole in this nation. There will never be another Dr. King, but his words will live on in our hearts: 'Free at last, free at last, thank God Almighty, we are free at last.'" Lisa finished reading her paper and looked up at the audience.

"Let's give her a hand," said Dr. Carter. "Thank you, Lisa."

The auditorium erupted in applause. Lisa looked at her parents, who had tears in their eyes. Ozella was grinning from ear to ear, and even baby Elizabeth was excited. The boys were jumping up and down.

Lisa then looked at Miss Loomis and Reverend Reed, who had tears in their eyes. Their applause meant the world to Lisa. It took courage for Miss Loomis to return to Wyatt to see Lisa. Lisa was Miss Loomis's shining star once again.

Chapter Twenty-one

The First Day

Lisa awoke, and anxious thoughts immediately flooded her brain. It was the first day of school at Elmwood Junior High, and Lisa felt like she was going to throw up. Then she remembered Miss Loomis and smiled.

"Please, God," prayed Lisa, "give Miss Loomis a great first day at Head Start."

Today was a special day for Miss Loomis. She was starting work as a teacher for the Montgomery Head Start program for underprivileged preschoolers.

Lisa looked over at the new plaid jumper and navy blouse that her mother had selected for her to wear today. Lisa got out of bed and began getting dressed. When she put on her padded bra, she noticed that it was tight. Her breasts had begun to grow, and they peeked out of her padded cups.

"I'm going to need a bigger bra soon," thought Lisa.

She then put on her blouse and jumper and looked at herself in her full-length mirror.

"Not bad," she thought as she started brushing her soft blonde hair. She pulled her bangs to one side and secured them with a tortoiseshell barrette.

Today was also a special day for Lisa. She would get to wear makeup for the first time. She had bought the Maybelline "Blooming Colors" eye shadow set for blue eyes, and she began applying light blue eye shadow to her upper eyelids. She then applied light pink eye shadow as an accent under her eyebrows. She learned this technique from the Maybelline ad in her *Seventeen* magazine. She then applied brown Yardley mascara to her eyelashes. It was hard to put on mascara for the first time. She would have to practice. She then put pink powdered blush on her cheeks, and she used her pinky finger to remove pink Yardley lip gloss from its tiny pot and apply it to her lips. Lisa's two blue eyes peeked out through her new makeup.

On the other side of town, Miss Loomis awoke, and anxious thoughts immediately flooded her brain. It was the first day of Head Start, and she felt like she was going to throw up. Then she thought of Lisa and smiled.

"Please, God," prayed Miss Loomis, "give Lisa a great first day at school, and let there be no mean boys."

She looked over at the new dress that she had selected to wear today. It was canary yellow with black piping. Miss Loomis got out of bed and began getting dressed. When she put on her padded bra, she noticed that it was loose.

"I'm going to need a smaller bra soon," thought Miss Loomis.

She then put on the new dress and looked at herself in her chifferobe mirror.

"Not bad," she thought as she put her wiry white hair

into a bun. She noticed that her hair was thinning even more and that there were more bald patches on her scalp. Two brown eyes peeked out from her thick white glasses.

And so the first day of school began. Lisa was growing while Miss Loomis was getting smaller. Lisa had graduated to the seventh grade while Miss Loomis was now teaching preschool. Lisa seemed to be going forward while Miss Loomis seemed to be going backward. Lisa no longer counted on Miss Loomis to make it through the school day. Reverend Reed no longer counted on Miss Loomis to help with the movement.

Miss Loomis was fast becoming her Macy's Thanksgiving Day balloon. The bullying and the movement exacted a heavy toll on Miss Loomis. She died on Halloween after being at Head Start for only two months. Like the helium of her balloon, her spirit rose to the promised land, and, like the shell of her balloon, her frail body fell to the earth. She was free at last.

In many ways Lisa grew from a child to a woman on the day that Miss Loomis had died. She had exposed her wounds to the world. She had survived the teasing on the playground. She had understood what a Negro teacher and a white girl with a cleft palate and cleft lip have in common. Lisa would never forget Miss Loomis.

That night Lisa dreamed of the Little White House of the Confederacy once again—yet things were oh-so-different in this dream. Now, there were no white crosses and servants' uniforms. Instead Lisa and Miss Loomis were dressed in their Sunday finery and were seated at the dining room table. Lisa no longer had cleft palate and cleft lip. Also seated at the table were Dr. Martin Luther King Jr. and Senator Bobby Kennedy. Governor Wallace was serving them slices of Miss Loomis's devil's food cake. Lisa noticed that the chocolate cake was so dark that it peeked through a veneer of thin white icing. Suddenly, Dr. King, Sen. Kennedy, and Miss Loomis turned into white doves. The doves began pecking at the window trying to get out. Lisa opened the window, and the three white doves flew outside.

Lisa awoke from her dream, touched her scars, and smiled. She could not wait for the morning.

Acknowledgments

To my sixth-grade English teacher, who taught me to be brave in the face of adversity; to Gloria Steinem, who taught me that law can be connected to justice; to the late Dr. Anthony Marzoni, who gave me a face; to my mother, Frances Lyles Harper, who taught me to speak; to my late father, Henry Johnson Harper, who taught me to love books; to my brothers, Henry Harper, Jr., and John Harper, and my sister, Millicent Harper Veltman, who taught me to love; to my friends Ruthie Rittenour Nesbitt, Ellie Scott Kirby, Betsy Garber, and Chris Dozier Thomas, who taught me how to be a friend; and last but not least to Debra and Mark Meehl, who taught me to believe in myself.

About the Author

photo credit: Debra Meehl

Leah Harper Bowron is a lawyer and James Joyce scholar. Her article "Coming of Age in Alabama: *Ex parte Devine* Abolishes the Tender Years Presumption" was published in the *Alabama Law Review*. She recently lectured on Joyce's novel *Ulysses* at the University of London and the Universite de Reims, and she is currently writing a book on a code that permeates the writings of James Joyce. She lives in Texas and has a daughter named Sarah and a cat named Jamie.

SELECTED TITLES FROM SPARKPRESS

SparkPress is an independent boutique publisher delivering high-quality, entertaining, and engaging content that enhances readers' lives, with a special focus on female-driven work. Visit us at www.gosparkpress.com

Beautiful Girl, by Fleur Philips. $15, 978-1-94071-647-3. When a freak car accident leaves the seventeen-year-old model, Melanie, with facial lacerations, her mother whisks her away to live in Montana for the summer until she makes a full recovery.

Girl Unmoored, by Jennifer Gooch Hummer. $15, 978-1-94071-607-7. It's 1985 in Maine, and Apron Bramhall is about to be saved by Jesus. Not that Jesus; the actor, Mike, who plays him in Jesus Christ Superstar. When he and his boyfriend Chad offer her a summer job, she uncovers Chad's secret, and starts to see things the adults around her fail to—like what love really means, and who is paying too much for it.

Bear Witness, by Melissa Clark. $15, 978-1-94071-675-6. What if you witnessed the kidnapping of your best friend? This is when life changed for twelve-year-old Paige Bellen. This book explores the aftermath of a crime in a small community, and what it means when tragedy colors the experience of being a young adult.

Crumble, by Fleur Philips. $15, 978-1-94071-611-4. Eighteen-year-old Sarah Mcknight has a secret. She's in love with David Brooks. Sarah is white. David is black. But Sarah's not the only one keeping secrets in the close-knit community of Kalispell, Montana.

The Revealed, by Jessica Hickam. $15, 978-1-94071-600-8. Lily Atwood lives in what used to be Washington, D.C. Her father is one of the most powerful men in the world, having been a vital part of rebuilding and reuniting humanity after the war that killed over five billion people. Now he's running to be one of its leaders.

About SparkPress

SparkPress is an independent, hybrid imprint focused on merging the best of the traditional publishing model with new and innovative strategies. We deliver high-quality, entertaining, and engaging content that enhances readers' lives. We are proud to bring to market a list of *New York Times* best-selling, award-winning, and debut authors who represent a wide array of genres, as well as our established, industry-wide reputation for creative, results-driven success in working with authors. SparkPress, a BookSparks imprint, is a division of SparkPoint Studio LLC.

Learn more at GoSparkPress.com